MB

GOLD OF THE PADRES

Simon Dawson, a mining engineer, is killed for his map of La Mina Del Padre—an old mine shaft in the hills reputedly filled with silver bullion and gold plate from Spanish missions, and jewels looted from Aztec temples. Deputy Lee Baxter and Sheriff Jon Thorne set out to track his killer—but Baxter, ex-outlaw and bank-robber, finds more than he bargained for in Anita Graham, a half-Ute beauty who has the map.

GOLD OF THE PADRES

Wes Yancey

A Lythway Book

CHIVERS PRESS
BATH

First published
by
Cleveland Publishing Co. Pty. Ltd.
This Large Print edition published by
Chivers Press
by arrangement with
the author
1991

ISBN 0 7451 1351 6

British Library Cataloguing in Publication Data

Yancey, Wes
  Gold of the padres.
  I. Title
  823.914 [F]

ISBN 0–7451–1351–6

CONTENTS

CHAPTER ONE

LEFT FOR DEAD

From where he stood on the rocky pinnacle, the Great Salt Desert seemed to stretch limitlessly, fading into the range of bluish hills that looked almost ghostly in outline in the far distance. Staring, he knew with grim satisfaction that he had Mick Magruder and the half-breed girl trapped.

They were down there, among the scattering of boulders that had been whitened and scoured by wind and rain for centuries. They were hiding, a hopeless move, because they were out of handgun ammunition, and probably water too, he guessed—and with a dead horse back in the gully.

He shouted, 'Come on out—hands reachin' for the sky. You're finished, Magruder—you and that half-breed Ute bitch!'

He waited. His harshly lined face, old-looking for his twenty-eight years, was masked with sweat and dust. There was weariness in his lean frame and no joy in his heart. He felt little triumph in the fact that so far he was the winner in this hunt for a killer and his girl.

He was about to call again when a man rose

1

from behind a large boulder and stared bitterly up the slope. He was a big fellow who would tower over most. He wore a dusty plaid shirt and a buckskin vest. His brown cord trousers clung to his thick thighs. His eyes were shaded by his battered fawn hat as he lifted his hands.

The girl followed his example. She seemed slight beside Magruder, but this was deceptive; she had a shapely figure and was of medium height. She was dressed in beaded buckskin from her shoulders to her moccasined feet, and her sleek black hair was covered with a purple silk bandanna with the exception of two long braids down her back. She was startlingly beautiful, even though travel dust stained her face.

Lee Baxter compressed his mouth to a tight slit as he studied the girl. He had never seen her before; he'd merely been handed instructions to hunt Magruder and the girl. But he'd seen the big man twice in town, both times in saloon brawls in which the hefty fellow had seemed bent on killing his opponent with his fists. A gun in the ribs and two separate spells in jail had been the only way to deal with the brawler. Then Mick Magruder had killed Simon Dawson. A big mistake.

Lee walked down the slope, his gun hip high. Nearing Magruder, he saw a sneer develop on the man's fleshy young face.

'You've got the drop on us, Deputy,'

2

Magruder said. 'But how d'you figure to get us back to Grass Valley? I mean, there's Anita here . . .'

'Maybe she'll ride a bit and maybe she'll walk a bit—it depends,' said Lee Baxter.

It was a signal for the fury in the girl's lovely face to express itself in angry words. 'You dirty lawman! You've dogged us for miles! You knew you were chasing us into a trap with these salt flats ahead and our horse lame for many miles.'

'So you speak English.' Lee stared curiously. 'I thought you were—'

'A reservation squaw!' she flashed. 'Sure, me speakum English!' The mocking comment was thick with hate. 'I probably speak it a damned sight better than you do, mister. My father educated me—but never mind that. You think you've got Mick heading for the gallows . . . well, it's a long way to Grass Valley and you could die somewhere along the trail, you two-cent badge-man!'

'I could let you try makin' it across the desert,' snapped Lee Baxter. 'You'll end up real dead—food for the buzzards—and that would save me some thankless work.'

'You lean, dirty apology for a lawman!' Her scream of fury came as she lost control and rushed forward, blind to the menace of his Colt. 'I've heard about you! Ex-outlaw—pardoned— now a badgetoter!' Fury blurred the rest of her outburst and then she was on Lee Baxter, her

3

fingernails clawing at his face.

This was no foolish onrush but a real attack, and had it come from Mick Magruder it would have earned a slug. But Lee hesitated. Case-hardened, with many scruples lost down backtrails which he now regretted, he saw the girl as one of the weaker sex—a mistake. She got close to him, blindly ignoring the gun. Her hands raked down his face before he jerked back. He dug in his heels as he retreated, then he holstered his gun. As the girl leaped again, Lee hit out, stung to retaliation. His hand flattened hard against her cheek, jerking her head back. She glared, her brown eyes showing the savage streak in her ancestry. She jumped forward again, one hand scraping deep into the flesh of his cheek, just missing tearing out his eye. Her other hand flashed to his gun.

Lee Baxter's experience with the scum of border towns for many years had cultivated a swift reaction when needed. And he had it now. The girl had enjoyed initial surprise. Now she'd have to pay.

He hit her hand away from the gun and then slammed a left hook to the side of her face. She swayed, eyes wide like those of a frightened animal. Lee swung his open palm—this time to her left ear. A thud and she crumpled to the ground, looking suddenly pitiful and small.

Mick Magruder didn't stand still. He went blindly at Lee Baxter just as the girl sagged.

4

Lee side-stepped and hit the man with a right and a left. Mick Magruder took the punches, staggered around in a boot-grating circle and came in again, fists windmilling. Lee knew he had a fight on his hands unless he backed away fast and pulled the gun.

Mick Magruder was big and heavy and he liked rough-houses. True, he had walked some miles in the searing heat, helping the girl and carrying a saddlebag. He was probably choking with thirst now, but he packed more weight than Lee. He suddenly jumped in and rammed a low punch to Lee's groin. Lee doubled over, gasping, a sour taste filling his mouth. In that moment of weakness, Mick Magruder followed up with his other fist into Lee's eyes. Hard knuckles ground and blood spurted from a torn eyebrow. Lee felt his senses swim. He dug in his heels for support. Then another blow came in, low again. Lee moaned sickly, unaware of anything except pain and nausea. Then he passed out.

When Lee regained consciousness, Mick Magruder had his Colt and was pointing it at his head with a wide, fleshy smile of triumph.

'You're licked, lawman. Anita did you in, bless her lovely hide. Now I'll have the pleasure of killing you.'

'You'll swing just the same, Magruder. Somebody will get you.'

'But it ain't gonna be you, Mr. Lee Baxter. It

seems your little spell with the law ain't had much of a work-out. You should have stuck to robbing banks with the Cready brothers. That pardon you got for saving Judge Barratt's life has just won you a quick ticket to hell. Seems you weren't meant to be a lawman.'

Seeing the finger whiten inside the trigger guard, Lee hastily decided to keep the man talking. 'Listen, you can go get my horse, you and the girl, and ride away. Just leave me here. You don't have to shoot me. You've got it all made—a gun and a horse—what more do you want?'

'You begging?' Magruder wanted to gloat.

'Grow up. What the hell good does killing do?'

'I've heard that you gunned down your share.'

'Only in self-defence. That came out at the hearing.'

'When you got that damned pardon? Good thing it was a judge you helped. It wouldn't have mattered a damn if it'd been some range tramp you saved.' Magruder rubbed the back of his left hand over his beard stubble. 'You've got to die. After all, I did Simon Dawson in...'

'Why, Magruder?'

'We had an argument.'

Lee eyed the gun again. 'I've been told that you and Simon were real pally for weeks. A queer combination because Simon Dawson was an educated man—an engineer of sorts.'

'A mining engineer,' said Magruder, and then he tightened his lips as if he regretted the admission.

'And you a rough-house galoot,' said Lee. 'What did you have in common? I didn't know this Dawson—only saw him briefly in town, but of course, I'm new to Grass Valley.'

'Damn you and all this talk,' snarled Mick Magruder 'You've got to die. You're in the way.'

Lee said. 'No. Just head out. You've got a gun and my horse is hitched in the rocks only twenty yards back. You and your Ute half-breed can skedaddle. Maybe you'd even reach Carson City. You'd just be one more wanted man among a whole parcel of 'em out there.'

'You ought to know ... outlaw!' sneered Mick Magruder. 'But I ain't heading for that part of the territory. I got other plans. I'll go to the hills—eastward.'

'Don't tell him anything, Mick,' said the girl quickly.

'You're right, honey-girl, even though he's gonna be buzzard meat.'

The girl's brown eyes flashed. 'Maybe we could just leave him ...' Her smooth face looked momentarily doubtful.

'Tell this man of yours to just leave me here,' Lee put in. 'Play it safe, miss. What's your name again?'

'Anita—my surname is Graham,' she said in her curiously well-modulated voice. Then her calmness vanished and anger sparked in her eyes as she saw the derision in Lee Baxter's face. 'My father is a teacher and my mother was half Ute. My grandmother was the daughter of a chief.'

'Graham ...' He grinned. 'A queer name for a Ute.'

Her fury rose. 'Don't you dare talk to me like that! I'm better than you, not worse. I never broke the law! You did, despite your pardon!'

'You're running off with a murderer. Magruder never gave Simon Dawson a chance.'

'How do you know? You weren't there.'

'I've been briefed.'

'It's all lies.' She walked close to Lee, her face tense with her dislike of him. 'It was a fair fight. Mick told me.'

'Then you didn't see it.'

'I believe Mick.' Her eyes blazed. 'He's good to me. He treats me like—like ...'

'You weren't part Ute,' Lee mocked.

Once again her hands streaked out to claw at him, but Lee Baxter turned his head and shoulders and avoided the attack. He didn't want any more of that. Blood was still trickling down his cheeks from the first assault.

'Keep back, Anita,' Mick Magruder warned and he shifted his stance, his eyes clashing with

8

Lee's wary gaze. 'Damn all this talk! Let's kill him, get his horse and ride out of this stinking heat.'

Under the buckskin her breasts were heaving with her anger. She certainly had a temper, a kind of primitive, uncontrollable thing that matched her hereditary background and her youth. For a moment, in sudden curiosity, Lee Baxter wondered what this beautiful girl saw in the loutish Magruder. She had to be fond of him to run away with him and place herself on the wrong side of the law. She was, in effect, helping a murderer escape justice.

Lee cursed inwardly. He had botched up his first important job as a deputy to Sheriff Jon Thorne, and that middle-aged worthy wouldn't lose any sleep if he never made it back to Grass Valley alive—although he wanted Mick Magruder for prestige reasons. Sheriff Thorne didn't like Lee; he was suspicious of him and resented the fact that he'd received a pardon. He didn't particularly want him as a deputy, and he'd known when he'd sent him out after Magruder that it could be a rough assignment.

The big man in the plaid shirt and buckskin vest raised the gun to firing position. 'This is it, Deputy.' The gun bucked.

Lee lunged to one side, willing himself to evade the bullet that roared from the Colt in Magruder's hand.

He didn't make it.

9

Something seared into his head. Blinding lights made vivid images behind his eyes and then he was falling.

Mick Magruder lowered the smoking gun. 'Let's get the hell out of here, Anita!' His voice sounded frightened. Although he had killed once, he was inwardly a coward.

A reai gunman would have turned Lee Baxter over. But Mick Magruder wanted only to leave the scene. He wanted to get away fast. He had felt the same way when Simon Dawson had died.

'He's—he's dead,' stammered the girl.

'Him or me!' The harsh reply hit the girl like a slap in the face. 'Let's move!'

She glanced at Magruder, wondering. He grasped her arm and dragged her a few yards up the rocky slope.

'Come on. Let's find that horse. The shot might have spooked it...'

They began to run, scrambling through the rocks, the white boulders that lay like gravestones on the alkali sand. In a few moments they had reached the ridge and then, as they went past a skull-like bluff, they saw the tethered horse. Its ears pricked as they ran towards it.

*   *   *

Lee Baxter lay as dead. Blood from his head

made a little pool in the sand. Some sand-flies appeared from nowhere and danced around the wound. An absolute silence fell over the scene.

He wasn't dead. His frantic leap for life had kept the bullet from exploding his skull. The slug had only creased him, stunning him and taking skin and flesh away. He lay there, still, the heat hammering down on him. His hat was half on his head and half off. The blood congealed under the heat, but a nerve throbbed steadily just beside his ear. When he finally moved, the pulse was like a hammer inside his head, pounding and pounding. His eyes shut, mouth open and sucking for air, he began to groan.

When he opened his eyes, his senses swam and he shut them again and almost wanted to die. But then the desire for survival made him open his eyes again—and keep them open—as he stared at the sand and pebbles inches from his gaze.

He stirred and struggled to stand up. He swayed like a drunk. He licked his lips and tried to spit, then he put a hand to his wound and looked at the sticky blood on his fingers. Finally a picture of Magruder pointing the gun came to his mind.

He tottered forward like an infant learning to walk, then fell again. On his hands and knees, he made his way up the slope and then lurched along the defile. He remembered the waterhole he had passed. Could he find it or would he lose his sense of direction as he staggered through this barren country?

After an hour-long lurching trek, he recognised some gaunt Joshua trees. The water was here—somewhere—in a rocky basin—easily overlooked—and probably Magruder and the girl hadn't seen it when they'd first passed this way.

Choking now from lack of water, he began to feel light-headed. He would have to rest, give his nervous system a chance to recover from the shock of the head wound, but he needed water.

For some delirious moments he thought he was mistaken in the location and he staggered this way and then that. Finally, he stumbled on the pool and gave a cry of relief. The water, which apparently seeped up from underground, was covered in a green slime. He skimmed it away, cupped the brownish water into his hands and brought it to his lips. After drinking, he took off his bandanna, soaked it and held the wet cloth to his head.

He rested until sundown, then walked on, mile after mile, taking his direction from the stars. The wind had already blown away the trail made by his horse the day before. Then, too tired to go on, he found a grassy hollow near some rocks and fell asleep.

He woke up feeling stiff and cold, aware that daylight was creeping over the land and that a man was standing over him.

'How come, Baxter?' said Sheriff Thorne unpleasantly. 'How come you let him best you? Or didn't you have the guts for it? Either way I figure you ain't got the makings of a lawman. Maybe I ought to take that badge back...'

CHAPTER TWO

RIDE FOR THE HILLS

The ride back to Grass Valley took all that day.
The sheriff's big bay plodded on under its
double burden. Conversation during the ride
was almost nil, and once, when Lee shared the
other man's food and coffee over quickly built
fires, the sheriff was openly hostile.

'Jumped you, did he? Then left you for
dead?'

'That's what I've told you.'

The sheriff stared into Lee's face. His big
walrus moustache didn't hide his sneer. 'Judge
Barratt made a mistake, mister, when he gave
you that pardon. He should have known better
than to insist I take you on. A hardcase doesn't
make a lawman. I followed you because I didn't
trust you.'

Lee grinned crookedly. 'I'm glad you didn't
trust me.'

'Smart, huh? But not smart enough to keep
Magruder at the right end of your gun.'

'I damn near died, Thorne. You figure that
was for fun?'

'You botched it. I'll tell Judge Barratt that.'

'Sure, enjoy yourself. Tell him how you don't
like ex-outlaws. Forget how many good sheriffs

14

were once on the wrong side of the law. And forget how many sheriffs have turned bad.'

'You robbed banks. That's straight damn thievery. I ain't robbed no person in my life. You expect me to shake your hand and tell you the robbing don't matter now?'

'I was young, crazy. I was all wrong. I admit it. I know I was lucky not to get caught and sent to the penitentiary. I also know it was a turning point for me when I saved the judge's life in that stagecoach holdup. I'm grateful for the chance he's given me. And now, Thorne, let's just close the subject. I've said all I'm gonna say. Just one more time—I'm sorry I didn't get Magruder and that girl.'

'What makes you think we're finished with him? We'll get a report on him sooner or later.'

Grass Valley was one of the few fertile areas in that western corner of Nevada, a place where sheepmen were taking over miles of hilly land and cattlemen clung to the valleys. Gold had been found in the river that flowed down from the hills and men had rushed into the area. The town of Grass Valley saw these placermen only on occasional weekends. So the community was a queer mixture of old and new. The settlers worked hard and lived clean, but the newcomers brought trouble. Cattlemen viewed the sheepherders suspiciously and sometimes fought with them. The gold-seekers got drunk and were robbed, and then sometimes they took the law into their own hands. So Sheriff Jon Thorne had gone through some rough times lately.

The day after he saw a doctor about his head wound, Lee Baxter returned to the sheriff's office. Thorne had news for him.

'That Magruder feller is up in the Indian Hills. Two gold-panners came into town and reported seein' him.'

'Were they sure it was Magruder?'

'He had this girl with him, sharing his horse. Can't make a mistake about that.'

'He's cut east,' said Lee. 'Well, he said he'd do that.'

'He told you that?'

'He yapped a bit. Said he wouldn't make for Carson City.'

The sheriff looked up from his desk. 'I'm gonna take you to see a gent who's stayin' at the Nugget Hotel. After we've had a talk, we'll see about riding out after Magruder.'

'You and me?'

'I want to keep an eye on you,' snapped Sheriff Thorne. 'We want to capture this killer and find out why he killed Simon Dawson.'

'They had an argument.'

'Sure, but about what?'

'You tell me, Sheriff.'

'Maybe we'll find out when we've talked to this gent.'

And that was all the sheriff would say until

they walked into the plush Nugget Hotel, when he grunted out, 'This feller we're seeing is called Dawson. Just got into town today by the morning stage. All the way from Twin Falls in Idaho . . .'

'Dawson?'

'Yep. He's Simon's brother and he sent a message that he wanted to see me.'

Dan Dawson, about thirty, was a well-dressed man who squinted behind gold-rimmed spectacles. He shook hands with the sheriff and then Lee as they met in the hotel lobby. 'I'm glad you've come,' he said.

'I hope we can help,' Thorne said. 'What did you want to talk about, Mr. Dawson?'

'My brother's death, of course. I feel sure his ridiculous ideas about that idiotic map and the lost treasure have something to do with his murder.'

Jon Thorne stared. 'I don't know anything about a map and a lost treasure.'

'You mean you haven't heard of the lost *La Mina Del Padre*? It's supposed to be somewhere in the eastern hills.'

The sheriff laughed. 'That old yarn! Nobody in these parts believes it.'

'I'm afraid my brother believed in it. He mentioned it twice in his letters to me.'

The sheriff grunted. 'Hell, there's always been stories of lost treasure, ever since the Indians started to attack the old Spanish

17

missions and the padres tried to hide their silver, gold and jewellery. Sure, there's treasure up in the Indian Hills—if you believe these old yarns. Hell, there's been stories of lost treasure from here to the Mex border.'

'True, but Simon was a mining engineer,' said Dawson curtly.

'You mean he had more than the ordinary man's knowledge of mine shafts,' put in Lee. 'Even so, locating lost caches is a tricky game. First there's the erosion of the land over the years, then there are the tricks wind and rain play with landmarks. I've heard about men going loco searching for treasure troves.'

'I've told you.' said Dan Dawson coldly. 'Simon had a *map*.'

Lee grinned. 'Yeah, I heard you. So?'

'I think he was killed for that map.'

Lee exchanged glances with the sheriff.

Thorne said, 'Mick Magruder, the man who shot your brother, was just a town brawler. He wouldn't know much about locating lost treasure.'

Lee Baxter sank to a red plush seat in the hotel lounge and said, 'Magruder and Simon Dawson were seen around town together quite a lot. You told me all about them, Sheriff, in your briefing before I rode out after Magruder.'

'Has the map been found in Simon's possessions?' asked Dan Dawson.

'Nothing like that was in his pockets,' said

18

the sheriff. 'And I never heard a thing about a map. But some of his gear is still in that room he rented from old Mrs. Cahill.'

'We must look through his belongings,' said Dawson.

'We'll do that right away,' Thorne agreed. 'And you'd better come with us.'

The old clapboard house belonging to Mrs. Cahill was only a few blocks away, around the corner from a livery stable. The grey-haired old Irishwoman showed the three men into a room Simon Dawson had occupied.

'I'll have to let this room again, Sheriff,' she said.

'I'll see that my brother's articles are taken away,' promised Dan Dawson. 'In the meantime, we'll look around if you don't mind.'

Apart from the bed and furnishings, there were two travelling trunks in a corner and a number of books stacked on a dresser. Lee Baxter thumbed through the books; most were about mining, geology and gold-extraction methods.

The trunks were not locked. Dan Dawson opened them. One contained only clothes and personal gear, and in the second one were notebooks. Dan Dawson took them out and the three men began to look through them.

There were sketches in the notebooks, mainly of derricks and tools. After nearly an hour in the room, there was nothing that resembled a map of the Indian Hills, but there were some pencilled notes about Mick Magruder. Lee Baxter found these notes and read them aloud:

'I regret hiring this man. He is bad-tempered and argumentative. I have told him too much about the La Mina Del Padre, the old mine shaft in the hills that was filled with silver bullion, gold plate and rawhide bags of jewels. In 1750, when the Apaches began plundering the missions in the Mojave Desert area the padres looked for some safe place to hide their treasures. They came far north, right to this corner of the Nevada Territory where the Ute Indians were peaceful. They wanted to hide the treasure in some place which would be located a year or two later, when it would be shipped to Spain. Their part of the New Mexico Territory was becoming too dangerous for the padres, what with robbing white desperadoes and the Apache who were learning that gold could buy them unlimited guns. I believe, from my investigations and studies over the past five years, that the shaft in the Indian Hills was filled with two thousand gold ingots, nine pack loads of gems that had been looted from Aztec temples, a few thousand bars of silver bullion and four religious codices smuggled from Spain when Spanish power was at its height—each worth its weight in diamonds. This loot was gathered from a number of missions in the New Mexico Territory, and carried off by mule train.

Now Magruder knows all this—and he has seen my map—a foolish thing for me to do, although I doubt if he could read the instructions properly. But I have a horrible feeling that he may have told another man—someone I call Mr. X for want of a better term—about my secrets. I must commit this to writing. I bitterly regret talking so freely to Magruder. At the start I considered he'd be useful—strong and ready to stand hardships in the hills while we looked for clues to the location.'

Lee stopped reading and looked at the other two men. 'That's it.'

'Don't that beat all!' said the sheriff.

'I knew he had researched deeply into this business,' said Dan Dawson. 'This confirms it. Quite frankly, I'm surprised he's given so much detail. He only dropped hints to me in his letters.'

'I can't see a map,' Lee pointed out. 'Plenty of sketches in these notebooks, but not one that resembles a map. How did he get such a map?'

'I have no idea,' admitted Dan Dawson. 'All I know is that these notes confirm my suspicions that Magruder killed my brother. I think you'll find that Magruder has this map.'

Lee walked to the window and then turned. 'Or maybe this Mr. X has it, huh?'

'Mr. X!' exploded Jon Thorne. 'By hell, that's all I need—a mystery man.'

'You will make further investigations,

Sheriff?' Dan Dawson asked.

'We're goin' out to look for Magruder.'

'I mean other details. For instance, did Simon buy any equipment? If he did, where was it taken? They may have obtained a shack somewhere and deposited gear in it. Maybe the map is there.'

Lee Baxter smiled into Dawson's face. 'Are you interested in justice or gold?'

'That is damned insolence!' Dawson snapped,.

'Your brother is dead,' Lee said sharply. 'Killed in a gunfight by a man he'd hired to do some work. The fight was seen by many others, so there's no doubt about who was the killer. By all accounts it wasn't a fair fight. Your brother didn't even pack a gun. That half-breed girl said it was fair, but I figure she's ready to believe anything Magruder says. Anyway, she didn't witness the fight. I'm telling you all this, Mr. Dawson, because capturing a killer is one thing and finding missing treasure is another. Matter of fact the latter ain't our business.'

Dawson's face twisted in anger. 'You two represent the law—and I expect you to find this Magruder.'

Lee turned away. 'Coming, Sheriff?'

Later, in the sheriff's office, Thorne turned from the window where he'd been standing in deep thought. 'Mr. X, huh? Now who did Magruder know in this town with brains and money—because it would take both.'

Lee just shook his head.

The rest of the day was spent in making inquiries of men Mick Magruder had known in town. They were much of a kind—good saloon customers who liked their drink and an argument. Lee Baxter and the sheriff worked their way through town separately, talking in saloons, near the stage depot where Magruder had been known to work when hard up, and at the stockyards where his type congregated. Neither mentioned anything about lost treasure or missing maps. They did ask if Mick Magruder had bought any mining tackle lately or had been seen moving gear out of town. The questions drew a blank. If Simon Dawson and Magruder had made such preparations, no one knew anything about them.

Lee and the sheriff met again to compare results

'Dead end,' said Lee. 'Sheriff, how long was Simon Dawson in Grass Valley before he died?'

'Just over three weeks,' said Jon Thorne promptly. 'Made it my business to find that out.'

'Three weeks. Not long.'

'He made at least two trips out to the Indian Hills—that much I did discover. He was seen twice in the area by a prospector, once ridin' alone and the second time with Mick Magruder.'

'Spying out the land,' mused Lee. 'You learned more than I did, Sheriff.'

'But not enough. We'll have to capture Magruder to get to the bottom of this. We'll ride out tomorrow at first light.'

They were ready the next morning with provisions for a four-day trip.

As their fresh mounts cantered out of town they attracted no visible attention except a stare from a freight-wagon driver who probably wondered why anyone else was out of bed so early.

But one man watched the departure of Sheriff Jon Thorne and his deputy from hiding, for he had received word the previous night that horses in the sheriff's livery were to be made ready for an early start and he was curious, guessing the purpose.

He was a heavy-set man with thick silver hair. He wore a good quality suit of blue serge. As the lawmen rode out he stood at the window of his apartment above the offices bearing the legend, CARL BEESON. PROPERTY & LAND ASSESSOR. INQUIRIES. The words were in gilt on a window painted a dark green so passersby couldn't see into the place. The door was of heavy pine with black iron hinges. The office was plain enough, with two desks, oak document cabinets and a hefty safe.

As the sheriff and deputy rode into the bright daylight, the man with silver hair slid his feet into riding boots, tucking his trousers into the handmade leather. He went along to the stable where his horse was ready. The hostler stood respectfully to one side, holding the bridle as the man mounted.

'Everything here, my man?' There was a nod and a gesture at the saddlebags, the water canteens, the rifle. 'As I ordered?'

'Everythin', Mr. Beeson. I done exactly as you said...'

'Keep an eye on the premises while I'm gone. Try the doors each night.'

'You figure to be away long, Mr. Beeson?'

'It depends. I might bring my business to a swift conclusion...'

He rode out. For an hour he kept to the trail Jon Thorne and Lee Baxter were using. They didn't see him; he wasn't that kind of fool. Then, after some miles of easy cantering, he left the trail where a stand of trees decorated a rising hill.

He had the advantage of the sheriff and the deputy in that he had more than a suspicion where he'd find Mick Magruder, and his route was a bit shorter than the well-used trail.

CHAPTER THREE

FURY OF THE FEMALE

It was inevitable that Magruder and Anita would have a fight. He had grabbed her arm, anger clouding his brain, and she had tried to break free. It was almost dark and the campfire burned brightly. Indian blankets were laid out on dry grass. They had had a tiring day of riding the hills, crossing endless ridges, back-tracking and staring at anything that resembled a rocky pinnacle. Now it was time to sleep—but Mick Magruder had other ideas.

'We'll sleep together,' he snarled. 'I aim to have you. This is the end of your fool act; standing me off like I was poison and you some kind of damn little queen.'

'No, Mick. We're not married. You said we'd get married.'

He stared disbelievingly. 'You little dope! How in hell can we get married out here in the hills? Now, come on Anita, you knew what to expect when we ran off together.'

'I will only sleep with the man who is my husband.'

But he kept a vice-like grip on her arm. He had treated her like a lady, and he'd stood off too long. A woman meant only one thing to

26

him. He'd take her that night and to hell with her scruples.

'You will have *me*,' he said.

'Don't try to use force,' she warned.

He was beginning to enjoy himself. 'Look here, girl, I'm used to getting my own way. Sure we'll get married—and we'll be rich, too, just like I told you. I've got the devil's own luck just now—I can feel it in my bones. We'll have more dinero than we can spend . . . as soon as I can figure out this damn map. But now . . .'

'No! Let me go!'

'Quit playin' around,' he snarled, then he began to draw her slender body against his.

She had allowed him to kiss her during the few weeks they had known each other, but she clung to the naive belief that he was in love with her and would take her as his legal wife. He had been nice to her most of the time, and on the few occasions when she had seen his temper flare, she had dismissed it as being part of his masculine nature. She admired his fine physique, his broad shoulders, the way he walked. If he bragged a bit, she thought it merely amusing. The shooting that had resulted in Simon Dawson's death had been bad, but it wasn't Mick's fault. It had been a fair fight—Mick had told her all about the way the man had insulted him. As for the deputy he'd shot, she'd had some bad dreams about that but reasoned that it had been a matter of survival.

'Leave me alone!' she cried now. 'Please, Mick!'

'Anita, we'll sleep together tonight because I say so.'

'I will not sleep with you!' She spat the reply and whipped a hand free. She groped for a stone on the ground. Her fingers cupped around one and then she jerked her hand around, aiming the stone at his head.

As he sought to hold her, the stone crashed against his skull. Magruder gave a cry of anguish and his senses swam. His grip on her weakened as he sat and swayed. Then she was on her feet, staring down angrily at him.

'Please : ... Mick ... we mustn't fight. I'm sorry ...'

Then, enraged, he shouted his real thoughts. 'You little Ute bitch! You damn squaw! I ought to kill you for that!'

She saw red as she heard the words she hated most. Ever since she had matured into womanhood men had eyed her with admiration while feeling contempt for her Indian heritage, and when she had rebuffed them they had resorted to the hated words.

'You can't talk to me like that!' Her screams tore into the night.

'This is where we quit foolin',' he rasped. 'I aim to take you, squaw bitch!'

He jumped up, hands reaching out for her. She leaped back, knowing she was defenceless

28

against this big man. She had no weapon, not even a knife. The solitary horse was tethered to a lightning-scarred tree some yards away. Mick Magruder had the rifle and gun that had belonged to the deputy. The saddlebag lay near the blankets. He had bought the latter from an Indian with the small amount of money he'd had on his person when they'd left Grass Valley. If she ran from him in this wild country, she'd be completely without resources. She tried again to plead with him, suddenly aware of her position.

'Mick, please don't touch me. Let's just sit down and talk about how we'll be rich when you find the treasure...'

He laughed nastily. 'When I find that mine shaft and the loot that was dumped there, I'll get any woman I want. In the meantime, honey, I don't mind being a squaw-man.'

Now her primitive fury rose to a new peak. She screamed insults in the Ute language she had absorbed as a young girl, in spite of the training her father had given her in the years after her mother had died.

He jumped at her, snarling. The blow on the head hadn't pleased him a bit. He'd teach her a lesson.

But she ran off, eluding him with a twist of her body when he caught up with her. She fled along the valley, running through scrub, avoiding thorny clumps of chaparral. He pounded behind her, yelling threats. On a straight patch of land he nearly caught her again, but she dodged away and headed for some boulders on a slope. Maybe he would give up, she thought. Maybe he would let her run into the wild land, expecting her to return when she realised she was without food or water.

She began to climb the boulder-littered slope, leaping from one rock to another. He roared out his rage and went after her.

Anita was still a few yards ahead of him. She heard his cries change to a shout of pain. She looked back, balanced on a boulder. Mick Magruder had fallen among the rocks.

She waited for a few seconds, sure he would claw out of the crevice into which he had slipped. But then she heard him moan in pain.

'Anita, I'm hurt. Get me outa here. Look what you've done to me.'

She went back cautiously and peered down at him. He lay on his back in a slot between the rocks, green prickly plants clawing at his clothes. He gave another moan as he saw her.

'My ankle! I've hurt it!' He tried to lever himself out of the narrow gap, his arms pushing at the boulders on each side. 'Get me outa here! C'mon, girl, lend me a hand.'

She stared at him impassively, her arms folded. 'I'm a squaw—a Ute bitch,' she said grimly. 'Remember?'

He struggled anew but his ankle was badly

30

twisted. He winced with pain and extended a hand. 'C'mon get me out of here. You do as I say, Anita. My damned ankle—maybe it's broke.'

'It could be a bad sprain,' she told him coldly. 'And if that's the case, you can hobble.' She turned away.

'Where in hell do you think you're goin'?'

'A horse is tethered back there,' she said. 'And there is food, water and guns. I believe the map of the lost mine is in the saddlebag.'

'You leave all that alone!'

'You forgot to call me a Ute bitch, didn't you?' she said sweetly.

He made an effort to claw himself out of the cleft. Finally his powerful arms prised his big body up and he fell flat over the rock, face down, groaning and gasping for air. Another twist and he was able to sit on the smooth boulder but his fleshy face was running with sweat because of the effort and pain. He ran a hand down to his ankle and cursed.

'Hell, it's swollen already!'

She said, 'Why did you kill that man Dawson?'

'I told you. We got into a fight—a fair fight.'

'But you took the map from him—or from his room.'

'From his room, Anita. Now, look—help me back to camp, eh. God, how am I gonna travel like this?'

'You killed Dawson thinking you could find the treasure yourself,' she stated calmly. 'I see it all now. I've been a fool over you.'

'I'll make it up to you,' he said. 'Wait'll you see that treasure, girl...'

'But we've searched all day for the pinnacle of rock that is supposed to be near the old mine shaft,' she said. 'We've had no success. I think you can't read that map.'

'I suppose you could do better.'

'At least I can read properly.'

'I can read, damn you!' he blustered.

'You make guesses. Now I'm going to study that map and see if I can understand it. So far you haven't let me see it. One thing I do not understand, Mick Magruder, and that is how Simon Dawson got hold of such a valuable map.'

'He told me he studied old Spanish documents in some big old mission that's a kind of museum, down at Casa Rio on the Mex border.' Mick Magruder smiled at the girl. 'All right, honey, I'll cut you in. I'll let you read the map; maybe you'll be luckier than me. Sure, you've got brains, and education, too. Yeah. Simon Dawson made that map—it's in his own handwriting. You might be able to figure it out better than me. I'll hand you that, gal. Now help me over to the camp.'

She backed sure-footedly over the boulders and left him. 'Thanks for all the information,

Mick. Adios.'

She turned and ran. He shouted after her. He struggled to reach another rock and snarled with the pain in his ankle. It would take him a long time to clear the rocky ground and traverse the flatter stretch. She would have plenty of time to fool him.

He cried out again. 'I'll kill you if you don't come back!' It was a ridiculous threat and he knew it. She turned and flung a taunting reply.

'I will be rich, white man, not you. I will find the treasure. You can perish for all I care. I hate you now.'

He struggled painfully to clear the rocks. He barely reached the grassy bank by the time she got to the horse. Hobbling, jumping along on one foot and grimacing with agony, he tried to cover some ground. She mounted the saddled horse and, with a mocking wave, rode calmly away into the night. She left him the fire. He tried to run, filled with a blind desire to kill this defiant girl, but he stumbled in his haste and fell to his hands and knees. When he got up again, Anita was gone.

He made it back to the fire in time and sank to the earth feeling murderous and a bit incredulous. He opened his mouth and bawled her name.

'Anita! Anita—a—a—a!' Echoes from the hills around flung his enraged words back at him. He stood up, tried to walk and knew he'd

33

get only a few yards. His ankle seemed on fire, tender and swollen. That wouldn't have mattered if he'd had a horse. By hell, he'd kill that bitch. She was too smart for a 'breed. She had the map and could read it, but all the same it wasn't possible for a girl to dig out the treasure even if she located the old shaft. So what made her think she had won?

As for Anita Graham, she rode carefully along a discernible trail for a number of miles and then when she saw the old caves high up the cliff face she halted. Magruder was many miles back and would never know which direction she had taken let alone catch up with her as long as he was on foot. She would have to rest. The day had been long and tiring.

The cliff face with its gargoyle sculptures looked eerie in the faint moonlight, but she was unafraid. They were the carved faces of Indians, cut out of the rock centuries ago by some forgotten race of cave dwellers. There were also the animals that were part man and part brute. The round cave mouth lay black and vacant.

She rode up, dismounted at the first convenient place and led the horse into the jagged hole. With the blankets wrapped around her and the rifle clutched in her arms, she lay down and fell into a troubled sleep. Her last thought was that tomorrow would bring new problems.

When the sun's pale fingers entered the Indian Hills area there were quite a number of people moving around. One of them was Carl Beeson, an impressive figure on his dapple grey horse. His suit showed no sign that he had camped for the night. He had shaved and washed in a stream and carefully dusted his clothes. He had polished his boots with a spare cloth he carried in his saddlebag. His pink face with its soft skin belied his age and was untroubled and calm. Authoritative and shrewd, with an appetite for wealth, which he was determined to amass somehow, he knew what his next step had to be. He must find Magruder. The man had doublecrossed him. Well, he would pay the penalty.

Carl Beeson rode slowly and carefully. He had prepared a good breakfast and had cleaned up after himself, hiding all signs of his campfire. He knew his way through the hills, having once partnered a prospector who had thought there was gold but was never lucky enough to strike it rich. Carl Beeson had quit roughing it and had turned to land and property speculation with some success. Knowing these hills was an asset. Having seen Simon Dawson's map he knew to within a mile or so where the old mine shaft should be and he thought he would find Mick Magruder and his girl in that area.

Of course, locating the actual spot of the filled-in mine shaft would be a laborious matter. He knew enough about these things to realise that land shapes changed over a century; that trees grew and rocky outcrops crumbled. Even pinpointing the location to a square mile would make the venture a matter of days and weeks of arduous searching.

He knew too well that he should have made a copy of the map, but it had not been in his keeping long enough. More important, he should have retained the map when he'd had the chance.

In any case he had planted the thought in Mick Magruder's mind to get rid of Simon Dawson. He had told Magruder that they could work together. He had not believed the big man would act so crudely as to shoot the other in front of witnesses and then make the fool play of running off with a girl—and the map.

The sun was rising quickly and promised another warm day, but a few clouds drifted low in the sky. The terrain was a series of ridges and hollows. Among some scrub oak groves he saw deer and smiled as they moved from his path.

He knew he would encounter some sign of the man—or the girl—pretty soon, and he had topped more than one high point in order to gain a view of a valley, but he was a little surprised when he saw the big man clinging to a tree and staring at him.

Carl Beeson rode up, keeping his right hand close to his belt. A small derringer was between the belt and his stomach. It was small enough to conceal but large enough to spit a nasty shot over a short distance. As he got closer to Mick Magruder, he saw that the man's holster was empty. He also noticed the way he limped and the wary expression on his face.

'Thought you'd be around,' said the silver-haired man. 'What's wrong with your foot?'

'It's broken, I think ... the ankle.'

'Where's the girl?'

'She ran off with all my things.'

'A quarrel, eh? Well, you don't need her. It was a stupid thing to do in any case. Why haul a girl around?'

'It ain't any of your damn business,' snarled Magruder.

'The map is my business. Where is it? I'm taking over this operation from now on. We'll work together. Brawn and brains, eh?'

'That Ute bitch ran off with everything,' Magruder said. 'The map is in the saddlebag.'

'Good God, you let her get away with it?'

'We were fighting. I slipped on a rock and—anyway, she went off last night. I've got nothing—no food or guns.'

'You have a talent for trouble, Magruder.

Not a good quality in a man. Well, now, so you haven't got the map. Interesting. It's in the possession of a mere girl.'

'I'll bust her up good, Beeson, then I'll get the map back. Just help me get my ankle bandaged...'

Carl Beeson shifted in his saddle. 'You botched everything. You shot Dawson in front of a crowd, then you ran off with a girl. You were then pursued by a deputy but apparently you triumphed there. The deputy, Lee Baxter, rode out of Grass Valley with the sheriff and—'

Magruder's eyes widened. 'He ain't dead? But I shot him.'

Carl Beeson nodded. 'I saw him with a bandage around his head. No, you didn't kill him. He and the sheriff are searching for you.'

'Blast their damn hides! Fix my ankle, Mr. Beeson, then we'll start lookin' for that lost treasure.'

'You are no further use to me,' said Carl Beeson, then he brought out the tiny silvery derringer. It bucked. Slowly, as Magruder stared in open-mouthed disbelief, a dark hole appeared in the centre of his forehead. Then blood welled out and the big man fell slowly, like a decayed tree trunk in a storm.

'The map,' murmured Carl Beeson. 'The girl ... I'll find her.'

CHAPTER FOUR

FIND MR. X

Lee Baxter and Jon Thorne rested their horses on the scrub-filled ridge and stared down into the steep ravine below, eyes fixed on the tents on the yellowish soil of the river bank. The gold panners were not ankle-deep in the shallow river as might be expected; they were congregated in a bunch on a flat part of the river bank. They were standing in a circle around Anita, yelling and cheering and laughing like maniacs.

'Hell's bells!' snarled the sheriff. 'Look at 'em! They're like damned animals!'

'I'm gonna stop it,' said Lee grimly.

'They won't like it,' Thorne said.

'You aim to come, or are you waitin' until they hurt her?' asked Lee caustically.

The sheriff touched his handgun. 'What in hell is she doing here alone anyway?'

'Let's find out.'

The placer miners were standing around the girl, jeering and yelling obscenities at her, making her dance. They had left their work and their tents when the girl had been spotted at the end of the ravine. She had ridden in, halted on seeing the placer camp and had tried to leave, but one big miner had grabbed the horse's reins and, laughing, had brought the protesting girl down the ravine. The rest of the men had been glad of a diversion from the everlasting panning and their obsession with gold.

'Dance, Injun gal! C'mon, show us a leg.'

'Hell, she's kinda pretty, ain't she, for a Ute?'

'Why don't she take off some clothes!' roared a wild-eyed man, his bare arms still wet from the river.

They were pushing her back into the circle. There was no escape. Her horse stood some distance away, cropping at some grass. The miners were not concerned with the animal; the girl was more interesting. They threw stones at her feet, compelling her to jump and, finally, dance. But it was obvious that the merriment would soon get out of hand. As Lee Baxter and the sheriff rode down, unnoticed by the men, the wild-eyed big fellow grabbed at the girl.

'C'mon, let's see if you're for real. I want to touch you.'

She fought but he held her. His hands tried to tug down the buckskin dress from her throat. The big man, aroused by the mere sight of a woman, thought she was fair game. The rest of the men jeered him on.

'Go to it, Red! Always knew you liked women.'

'Hell, Red, are you a squaw-man?'

Lee Baxter jabbed his horse into a sprint. He rode his big bay into the circle of placermen, thrusting them to one side. His gun was in his hand and he moved it in an arc. Yells of protest came from the throats of the men. The big, red-haired man holding Anita had more to say than the rest.

'Who the hell d'you think you are, lawman? You don't scare me none.'

'Let go of that girl.'

'You gonna make me?'

The man held the girl even more firmly, his arms around her, grinding his hands into her breasts although she struggled furiously.

Lee Baxter leaned over from his saddle, turned his gun swiftly in his hand and struck the red-headed miner a neat blow on the side of his head. The man released the girl and stepped back, stunned, then he glared defiance at the deputy.

'By hell, you can't do that to Red Wylie!' And the man rushed at Lee, grabbed his foot and hauled it clear of the stirrup. Then, with a terrific heave, he toppled Lee Baxter from the saddle.

Sheriff Jon Thorne was on the outside of the circle of men. He waited, hand on his gun, wondering if Lee could finish what he'd started. A sarcastic smile on his face revealed that he wouldn't be bothered too much if Lee received a hiding; on the other hand, he needed the

41

deputy to bolster his own authority.

Lee had dropped his gun in falling. He jerked back just in time to evade a big boot aimed at his head. The owner of the big foot staggered a bit as he tried to regain his balance. Lee jumped up and rammed a one-two into the man's face.

A roar of approval came from a dozen throats. This was entertainment, a fine relief from the drudgery along the river.

Lee faced a furious opponent. The two thumps into Red's whiskery visage had only inflamed the man's temper. He came in ready to hammer Lee into a pulp, throwing wild punches. Lee backed away and blocked two swings with his right arm. The circle of men parted to allow the combatants room. Lee retreated under the barrage of flailing fists.

Jon Thorne sat his horse, his face tightly set. The girl had moved away from the men, but she watched the fight as though fascinated. Lee's horse had shied away from the melee and stood, nostrils twitching, eyes gleaming.

Lee Baxter blocked another fist and then punched straight at Red's face with his right. The powerful punch was followed by a left that had all Lee's weight and power in it, his shoulders following through. Red rocked on his heels and Lee lurched in again, knowing he had to keep pounding this big man. He punched to the head and face repeatedly as Red's arms

42

hung helplessly. Finally the man went down.

The yells of encouragement stopped. The miners glanced at each other. One said angrily, 'Say, lawman, what's this to you, anyway? We was just havin' some fun with this Indian gal.'

Lee looked around for his Colt and saw it almost buried in wet sand. He picked it up. It would need cleaning. He sent a glance at Jon Thorne, who slid his gun from its holster and covered the crowd. He held the horse's reins easily, keeping the animal facing them.

'All right,' Thorne said authoritatively. 'Show's over. You boys can drift—before I run you in for assaulting this girl and brawling.'

The men began to walk away, grumbling uncomplimentary remarks about the parentage of most badgetoters.

Red Wylie got to his hands and knees and finally to his feet, lurching a bit and glaring at the man who had beaten him. He seemed about to rush in again, but he contented himself with spitting blood at Lee's feet before he tramped off.

Jon Thorne sighed in relief as he watched the ragged bunch of gold hunters drift down the ravine to their tents and working claims. Then he sent a glance at the girl as Lee strode across to face her.

'Where's Magruder?' Lee asked.

She looked at him in wonder. 'You should be dead.'

'That's been said to me before. Where is he?'

'I—I ran away from him...'

'Took his horse, too. How did you manage that?'

'We had a fight.'

Lee tapped her buckskin-clad arm impatiently. 'Now, come on. I don't aim to drag it out of you. We want Magruder. He's a killer, remember.'

'Then you'd better look for him.' Again there was defiance in her brown eyes. She gave a little jerk of her head and her twin braids of black hair settled down her back. He saw the resentment and at the same time the loveliness of her face and knew she was waiting for him to say the wrong thing. Well, there would be no sneering remarks from him about her mixed blood or the fact that she had run away with a man.

'You had a fight with Magruder—and beat him?' he asked. 'What happened?'

'He tried to force himself on me.'

The sheriff's sarcastic voice cut in. 'What did you expect, Miss Graham?' He put emphasis on the last two words.

Lee turned on the older man. 'Cut it out, Thorne.'

The sheriff glared back. 'Respect my authority, Baxter.'

'I'm trying, mister.' Lee turned back to the girl. 'We want Magruder, not you. I'm willin'

44

to forget that you helped him when he near killed me. Just describe the place where you left him.'

'Miles away—past the Indian caves. He had hurt his ankle and couldn't run after me.'

'So that's how you got away from him. Right. I think the best thing is to take you along, then you can point out the spot where you left lover-boy.'

She flashed her reply. 'He wasn't my lover.'

'You ran off with him.'

'I did not allow him to make love to me.'

'Liars, all of 'em,' grunted Jon Thorne. 'Never met a Ute who didn't lie and steal.'

Anita jumped at him and hammered her fists at his leg. The horse shied away. Jon Thorne rasped angrily in his throat and tried to swing a hand at the girl. Lee grasped her arm and pulled her back. She turned on him as if she wanted someone to vent her fury on.

'Let me go.' She pounded her small fists against his chest. He took her hands and gripped them so tightly the skin went white.

'I've had you claw my face once,' he snapped. 'It ain't gonna happen again. Calm down, you she-cat.'

'He did not make love to me!' she screamed. 'And I am glad because he is a pig. You understand? A pig! A white pig!'

Lee held her until her anger subsided. Then he said to the sheriff. 'Get her horse. We'll ride

45

back. Might be the best way to find Magruder.'

When they finally got the girl into the saddle she seemed composed, and the ride back over the first few miles was devoid of tantrums. Lee took the opportunity to question Anita.

'What do you know about Mick Magruder apart from the fact that he killed Simon Dawson and is wanted for murder?' He paused and said casually, 'Did you know Dawson had some strange ideas about finding a treasure in the hills?'

'Treasure?'

'You lived in these parts,' he said. 'You must have heard about the tales of the padres who, ages ago, fled up here from the south and buried their loot in an old mine shaft.'

'Oh, that ancient story...'

'Yeah, Anita, *that* story. Simon Dawson hired Magruder to work for him. They argued and Magruder killed him. That much is certain. We think Mick Magruder took a map from Dawson's room and went to look for the treasure. Now, how much did Mick tell you?'

'Nothing.'

'You didn't see a map?'

She held the reins tightly and smiled as she rode beside him. 'You don't really believe that Mick would tell me anything important? A mere girl ... a Ute...'

'You're more white than Ute,' Lee said. 'And you're an educated woman.'

'I am only eighteen.'

She sat in the saddle regally, her back straight, the reins in one hand. The buckskin skirt was parted and hitched up to show her tanned bare legs, but her male position on the saddle did not perturb her in the least. There was grace in her bearing and no shame at showing her legs. There was travel dust on her face, but even this did not detract from her dignity. Suddenly, for no rational reason, he felt glad that Magruder had not been her lover. He believed her.

'Being more white than Ute is important?' Her verbal thrust mocked him, cutting into his thoughts.

'I didn't really mean that. But you had a father who was a teacher.'

'Imagine you remembering that.'

They rode on—to find Mick Magruder lying dead under a tree, the hole in his forehead caked with ants.

Lee turned the man over and went through his pockets. 'No map, Sheriff.'

Jon Thorne glanced at the girl. 'She killed him.'

Anita was staring wide-eyed at the man who only twenty-four hours ago had sworn his affection for her and had promised her she would be rich. At Thorne's comment, a glint came into her eyes. 'I did not kill him.'

'You had a gun. You said you rode off with

everything he had.'

'The handgun is still in the saddlebag.'

Lee Baxter bent over the dead man again and studied the small round hole in his forehead. He was so long in the examination that the sheriff rapped irritably:

'What in hell are you lookin' at, Deputy?'

'This man wasn't killed by a Colt.'

'How do you know that?'

'The hole is too small. A Colt would tear out a bigger part of bone. Magruder had the Colt he took from me. If this girl has that gun, she couldn't have killed Magruder with it.'

'I reckon we should take a look in her saddlebags,' Thorne said.

'My saddlebags,' Lee corrected. Then, to Anita, 'Down, miss.'

She dismounted and stood silently while they went through the contents of the saddlebags. The handgun was there and Lee checked it, noting the cylinder was full. Apart from some food such as the dried meat Magruder had bought from the Indians, there was little else of consequence.

Anita had no intention of telling them that the map lay inside her buckskin dress. Already the idea had formed in her mind that if anybody was to be rich it might as well be herself. It savoured of justice, and of revenge on the white people.

'We've got to take this body back to town,'

48

grunted the sheriff. 'It's evidence. We'll get the doc to examine that bullet hole, too.'

'We'll need a horse for that.'

'She can double up with one of us.'

Lee grinned at the girl. 'You can ride behind me. Magruder will take the trail back tied over the other horse.'

Thorne glanced around. 'If she didn't kill him, there's a whole pack of questions that need answers.'

'Such as?'

'Who wanted Magruder dead?'

Lee looked at the girl again. 'Do you know anything? Were you followed? Did you see anybody at all?'

She shook her head. 'We stopped to buy food and blankets from some Indians. That's all.'

'When you ran off and left him it was dark?'

'I've told you that once already!'

'Don't snap at me, Anita. Don't you want to know who killed Mick Magruder?'

'I'm not really interested.'

Lee said, 'You backed him all the way when I tracked you two down to the salt flats. You flew at me, helped him beat me. What happened for you to change your mind about him?'

'He—he began to treat me bad.'

'You ain't explainin' much.'

'I'm a girl, aren't I?' said Anita fiercely. 'And he was a man—a rough man. Do you need to know any more?'

49

'You repulsed him?'

'That's one way to say it.'

He stood silently, for the moment glad of her answer although he didn't know why. She kept flicking curious glances at him, as if aware of his masculine personality but resenting it. She was not pleased with him in any way. She felt nothing but hostility towards him.

'Well, we've got one dead man,' grunted Jon Thorne. 'Plus one girl and a damn mystery. If she didn't kill him, then there's some murdering devil at large who did.'

Lee's brain suddenly flicked back over the notes he had read in Simon Dawson's handwriting. He said, 'Remember the "Mr. X" Simon Dawson mentioned in his notes, Sheriff? Well, maybe there is a Mr. X. And maybe he killed Magruder.'

The two men stared around the high wooded ridges that sloped into the valley. Even the girl was disturbed as she threw keen looks at the silent hills.

The sheriff turned back to her. 'Did Magruder say anything about another man?'

'Just Simon Dawson. I suggest you start working on it, Sheriff. Don't ask me to do your work.'

'Why, you little Ute bitch!'

She glared at him, contempt in her thin smile. Suddenly the paper under her dress felt good, satisfying. If there was any truth in the old treasure story, she might be the one to secure the reward. She would need help, that was certain. A lone girl in these hills was just asking for trouble. And someone had killed Magruder. She would have to be careful or she might be the next victim.

CHAPTER FIVE

TWO INTRUDERS

When they were finally ready for the ride back to Grass Valley and the civilised trappings of the town, they were three oddly assorted people. Sheriff Jon Thorne was glad he could present the body of the killer of Simon Dawson to the town committee, although this posed the question of who had killed Magruder and why. Lee Baxter couldn't forget Dawson's reference to 'Mr. X'. As for Anita, she was pleased with herself. The two lawmen had searched Magruder's pockets and the horse's saddlebags, but so far they didn't suspect that she had the map.

For a long time they were watched by a man who took care not to show himself or get close.

Carl Beeson's pinkish face showed annoyance every time he rode his horse to a crest and watched the distant riders. The girl rode double with the deputy. He could see the body of Mick Magruder slung over a horse.

His mind was obsessed now with thoughts of the treasure map. He had to get it. Who had it? The girl or the lawmen? But maybe the two men didn't even know of the existence of the map. He wasn't sure, but he knew that Baxter and Thorne had searched Simon Dawson's room. A spy had brought this information to him, but he could not guess at exactly how much they had learned about Dawson's plans. Still, the lawmen were smart enough to find out things. So maybe they did know about the treasure map. In that case, they might have it. On the other hand, maybe the girl had the map. She had been told enough about the treasure by the big fool, Magruder. Surely she would have looked for the map before she left him. Yes, that had to be the answer. The girl had the map. She would probably hide it from the lawmen. She was part Ute and cunning, like all that breed. It was a good bet that this slip of a girl held the key to a huge fortune.

Carl Beeson could only watch the three distant riders. Short of killing them, what else could he do? He had a rifle in his saddle scabbard, but he wasn't much good at long-distance shooting.

It was tempting to consider that he could retrieve the map if he killed the three, but was it practical?

He decided against it. A smoother way to operate would be to find out who had the map and then make plans to take it.

The sun was sinking over the distant horizon when the two lawmen rode into town with the girl and the dead man.

They didn't know that another rider came

into Grass Valley by an alternate trail, a man obsessed with the thought of fantastic riches. Carl Beeson mingled with a few other mounted men: ranchhands coming into town for a drink and some poker, a freight wagon on its last lap, and a gig carrying a man and his woman into town for a social event.

Mick Magruder was laid out in the mortuary. Lee and John Thorne went into the eating house and ordered steak. They had left the girl to go to her home. Jon Thorne knew she lived with her father, Gilbert Graham, in a small house near the town school. Her father would have to deal with the errant girl, a task probably beyond him because of his ill health. He was about sixty, having taken a young wife; but Anita's mother was dead now. How Gilbert Graham would deal with Anita, when he learned she had run off with Magruder, was anybody's guess. That part didn't really concern the law.

That night, after he had spent some time in the room he rented in town, Lee Baxter got rid of the bandage around his head. He bathed, then he got into fresh clothes and shaved. Finally he went to the nearest saloon and downed two shots of whisky. The whisky warm in him, he went to Mrs. Cahill's house to examine Simon Dawson's room again.

'You won't be long, will you?' asked the old lady. 'I've got another boarder coming to take over the place.'

The papers of the late Simon Dawson had not been taken away by his brother Dan. Lee began to read them again, wondering if there might be other references to 'Mr. X'. He was hoping for a clue, however faint.

But a fresh reading of the notebooks and slips of paper revealed nothing new. Lee re-read the passages about the lost gold and silver and wondered how Simon Dawson had been able to find a map to this legendary fortune. After all, a drawing with fairly precise details of location wasn't something that could be picked up by just anybody, otherwise the loot would have been discovered long ago. It seemed that Simon Dawson had been doing a little digging himself—in paper.

Lee was reading when the door opened and Dan Dawson walked in. 'Brushing up on the history, Baxter?' he said.

'I'm looking for some sort of clue to the man your brother called "Mr. X".'

'Is that a fact? Well, I'll take charge of these belongings of my brother's. That's why I'm here.'

Lee nodded. 'I guess you're entitled to them.'

'I hear you've brought in the body of Magruder. Who killed him?'

'We don't know.'

'It could have been that Indian girl.'

'Nope ... she didn't shoot Magruder. Maybe

"Mr. X" did.'

'The map. Did you find that?'

'It wasn't on Magruder, and it wasn't in the saddlebags.'

'The girl must have it!'

Lee stared and then felt a hot flush creep into his cheeks.

'You two law officers didn't consider that?' Dan Dawson's eyes were contemptuous behind the gold-rimmed glasses.

'We figured everything the girl owned was in the saddlebags,' Lee ground out. 'She denied knowing anything about a map.'

'And you believed *her*—an Indian girl?'

Lee Baxter clenched his fists. 'We did, and if you've got a complaint to make, hand it in to the sheriff.'

The other man began gathering up the notebooks. 'I certainly will see Sheriff Thorne about this. I think Magruder had the map.'

'Are you still hankering to find the treasure?'

'I think my brother would have wished me to take up his quest.'

The whole thing would be just a crazy idea,' said Lee, wishing to annoy this cold, humourless man.

'I'll be able to judge that when I find the map.'

Lee Baxter left the house with Dawson, there being no point in staying now that Dan Dawson had all the notebooks. In the street, he left

56

Dawson and walked slowly along the main stem where the lanterns cast yellow pools of light on the hard-baked earth. Grass Valley was coming to life for the evening round of entertainment. The saloons were full of noisy men and card games were getting into stride.

Lee Baxter couldn't forget the lovely oval face of Anita Graham. For some reason, as he walked deep in thought his footsteps took him up the slight hill to the east of town where the schoolhouse stood. Near the darkened building was the clapboard house which was the home of Anita's father. Jon Thorne had told him that this was where Anita lived.

Lee wondered if she would receive him in a friendly manner. Then he heard the scream that came from inside the house.

He sprinted to the verandah that ran around the house. The door was open slightly, and he saw the gleam of lamplight at the bottom of a passage, then he heard voice.

As Lee Baxter strode into the hall, the girl cried out again. 'No! Please, don't hurt him. I'll tell you.'

A male voice snarled, 'You'd better! And scream again, and we'll bust him!'

Lee Baxter whipped out his gun and took three fast steps to the door that gave access to the room. As he moved, a man said throatily, 'C'mon. We ain't got all the time in the world. Where is it?'

Lee made his entrance then, pushing the door in so hard it was nearly torn off its hinges. The two men and the girl jerked around.

There was a third man. He sat slumped in a cane chair, his grey hair like an untidy mop, his eyes closed. Blood ran from his nose and there was a cut at one corner of his mouth.

Lee Baxter had the drop on the two men. They were typical frontier men in dirty range garb. One man had the smell of the stockyards in the scuffed leather pants he wore. He was a small man, bald and paunchy. The other had a wary expression and a long nose.

'Freeze!' said Lee. 'Anita, what's it all about?'

She had a fast-working brain. 'They're dirty thieves, that's all.'

'I heard them talking. What do they want?'

'They just broke in.' The girl swallowed, unable to meet his gaze.

'For no reason?'

'I'm the reason,' she said. 'A girl, a Ute is fair game, as you well know by now.'

'That's not the truth. One of them was asking for something. They've hurt your father. They were punishing him, hoping to make you talk. Ain't that it?'

'I—I don't know what you're getting at.'

'The map, Anita,' he said. His gun moved to cover both men. 'I'll bet they were asking about the map.' Lee flashed a threatening look at the two men. 'All right, who sent you?'

Then Gilbert Graham gave a groan and opened his eyes. Anita bent over him and brushed strands of hair from his face. At that moment the taller of the two range tramps decided to jump at Lee Baxter.

Lee could have shot him dead, but he reversed his gun with a swift motion and cracked the man neatly on the head with the butt as he charged.

The man moaned and sank to the floor, and at that point the small balding man made his bid to escape. He rushed for the rear door as Lee dealt with his companion. Lee was in fact supporting the unconscious man's body, his gun in his hand, held by the butt, ready again for action.

As the smaller man heaved the door open, Lee jerked his attention to him. The small man whipped the door open and Lee fired.

The shot nicked the door frame. Then the man was gone.

Lee Baxter dropped the hardcase he was holding and dived after the escapee, shouldering past the half-open door into the darkness outside. He dived around the corner of the building, not sure where the other man had gone. Then he saw the fellow running as swiftly as his short legs would allow towards the darkness between a pair of two-storey buildings.

Lee gritted his teeth, knowing in that second that he'd have to kill the man or let him go. He whipped up his gun again and aimed.

But another gun beat him to it. The shot cracked into the night air and Lee saw the little man fall.

Lee ran swiftly, zig-zagging in case the attacker decided to snap a shot at him. If gunflame came from the darkness he was ready to pump a slug in that direction. But no gun barked. Lee reached the little drifter and bent over him. As Lee turned him over, he saw the sticky red patch on his shirt. The man's torn heart had pumped out its last blood.

Lee jumped up, knowing he was a prime target if the killer figured to chance another shot. He backed to the brick base of the two-storey building and waited. No sound came to his ears. Whoever had killed the small drifter was gone.

He had to get back to Anita and her father.

He burst into the house again and was just in time to prevent more trouble. The tall man was on his feet, his expression ugly. Anita was staring angrily at him, still bent over her father. As Lee entered the room, the man tried to get past to the other door. But Lee got to him, grabbed him and disarmed him.

'All right—talk. Who sent you?'

'You got it all wrong.'

Lee hit the man in the stomach. 'Some feller

paid you two to come here. What did he want you to get?' Lee held a fist in the man's face.

'A map. He said the girl had a map.'

'Where were you to take the map?'

'He said he'd see us down by the stockyard and pay us.'

'What does this man look like? Come on, I want a description.'

The man with the long nose scowled. 'How in hell should I know?'

'You saw him, didn't you?'

'I saw a galoot with a silk bandanna over his face. All I could see was his hat.'

'What colour?'

'Black, I guess. But new ... a good hat.'

'What sort of clothes? Good? Range gear?'

'No. He was in a suit. But, hell it was dark. I don't know anything more. Lemme go.'

'No chance!' snapped Lee. 'You're for jail. You broke in here, assaulted this man and terrified this girl. You'll stand in front of Judge Barratt. But you're lucky, mister. Your pal is dead.'

'You—you killed him?'

'No. Somebody was waiting outside, apparently not trusting you two to do the job properly. Your friend is dead, feller—shot by the man who hired you is my guess. Now does that inspire you to talk a bit more?'

'The goddamn skunk! Killed old Pete! But I—I don't know any more about the man. Pete

61

and me just met up with him on the boardwalk. We came out of the saloon—and there was this galoot.'

'Probably he'd observed you two for some time—or maybe knew something about you—and decided you'd do the job and no questions asked. Then although he'd arranged to meet you at the stockyard and pay you, he figured to keep a lookout just in case anything went wrong.'

Lee turned to Anita and asked her if she had any rope in the house. She nodded and left her father's side. She returned from the kitchen with a length of rope that Lee used to bind his prisoner's hands behind his back.

Gilbert Graham was able to look around and stare dazedly at the deputy. 'Anita, what's all this about? Those men—why?'

Lee Baxter grabbed his prisoner. 'I'm taking him to jail, Miss Graham. I'll be back—with questions.'

'I can't stop you,' she said. She stood in the cosy room, her Indian-style buckskin oddly at variance with the solid furniture. Two oak rocking chairs were on either side of the stone fireplace. A yellow photograph stood on the top of a thick mahogany dresser, showing the head and shoulders of a woman whose Indian ancestry was as marked as that in the face of Anita Graham.

Lee Baxter put his man behind bars. Then he

tramped back up the hill to the house beside the school, warily, because now it was obvious that 'Mr. X' was a very real person.

The night air was cool on his face as he pushed open the front door and walked into the house. He expected to see Anita attending to her father, as he had left them.

But there was another man present, a tall, handsome young fellow in Ute buckskin, a red-checked shirt and a fancy vest that would have been more suitable on a card-sharp. Dark hair, oiled and sleek, was piled thick on the young man's head. His black eyes glittered and there was distrust in his face. Lee knew at once that he was a half-breed Ute, but he'd never seen him before. He carried a gun in a yellow holster. The belt was wide and new.

Anita said, 'Deputy, this is my friend, Jesse Bridger. I've known him for some time.'

CHAPTER SIX

'THE GIRL HAS GONE OFF!'

In the apartment above the office bearing the sign, CARL BEESON. PROPERTY & LAND ASSESSOR. INQUIRIES, a man stood at the window and scowled into the night. His plans weren't going very well. He had been forced to kill. The act of murder didn't bother him; but, years back, before he came to Grass Valley, he'd left a big town to the north after shooting a man in the back. The town marshal had got too nosy, although he'd had no proof. Land speculation could be carried on anywhere in the booming western territories, so the move to Grass Valley posed no problems. He had brought capital with him. But now there was an incredible furtune out in the Indian Hills, lost for over a hundred years.

Carl Beeson had no doubt that the treasure existed. There had always been tales of it, handed down as folklore. And he trusted the sincerity of Simon Dawson, although he hadn't had any contact with the man. He was sure Dawson had been no crank.

Now he wished he'd made a copy of the map when Magruder had it. Instead, like a fool, he'd let the man retain it. Sure, he had intended to get possession of it within a day, but then the big lout had ridden out of town after shooting Simon Dawson.

Now his latest try to get the map had failed owing to a deputy who had no right to be so damned busy. Carl Beeson scowled again, his pink face showing anger. He had hired two stupid saloon wasters to do an important job. He would have preferred to do it himself, but he had to keep in the background. Nobody knew of his relationship with Mick Magruder. That was good; it meant he could operate freely. He wanted to keep it that way.

He was still backing his hunch that the girl had possession of the vital map. How long could she keep it? He was amazed that the two lawmen had not locked the girl up as an accomplice. And now the deputy had jailed one of the hirelings. Well, the man could tell little, and the other was dead. He had killed the no-account man on impulse, acting on the belief that a dead man was the best keeper of secrets. Maybe it had been unnecessary, for the man knew little, like his partner.

Still hugging the conviction that the girl had the map and had fooled the two lawmen, he left his rooms, locking the doors carefully. He felt the need for a drink in some quiet spot where he could think.

As he walked along to the one luxury hotel in Grass Valley, where he was a regular customer in the comfortable lounge, Carl Beeson could think of little else but the treasure. It haunted him. He had listened to the tales Mick Magruder had told him; tales that were a repeat of the stories the garrulous Simon Dawson had told the man. All he had to do was locate the old mine shaft which the padres had used to hide their treasure. He thought of the two thousand gold ingots lying behind a barrier of clay—which was how the shaft had been sealed. And nine loads of gems were in rawhide bags awaiting the light of day in order to gleam again. All that and silver, too. This vast wealth was somewhere in the Indian Hills. And the key to its possession was the map. To think that a slip of a girl had the map! God, he'd get his hands on it!

He walked into the Regent Hotel, still deep in thought, and ordered his favourite brand of whisky, shipped all the way from Scotland. He carefully poured the liquid. This very drink had originated in a faraway land, where icy mountain streams trickled through heather-clad hills and the local water possibly gave the scotch whisky a fragrance no other brew could obtain. Time and distance! These same qualities applied to the treasure of the padres.

He was aware of the other man who sat alone at a mahogany table going through some notebooks. The man's gold-rimmed spectacles glinted in the light of a nearby lamp. His fawn suit was of good cut and undoubtedly tailored in some big city. Soon Carl Beeson realised the identity of this man. His spies had told him that a man named Dawson had arrived by stage from Twin Falls, Idaho. Simon's brother.

This prim-looking man wasn't very much like the Simon Dawson Carl Beeson remembered. There was some resemblance in build, but not facially. Not that that mattered. What was important was Beeson's notion that Dan Dawson had to be interested in his brother's research. What kind of notebook was he studying so intently? He had two notebooks, and there were some loose slips of paper. Even from here, he could discern outlines of drawings on the pieces of paper.

Picking up his glass and the bottle of whisky, Beeson walked casually over to Dawson's table and stood there, smiling. 'Excuse me, you're Dan Dawson, aren't you. The brother of that poor young fellow who was murdered. It's the talk of the town.'

Dan Dawson looked up. 'Yes, I'm Dawson. But, if you don't mind—'

'Allow me to introduce myself. I am Carl Beeson, land and property buyer.'

'Am I supposed to find that interesting?' Dawson gathered up his papers and the two notebooks but not before the other man's keen eyes had seen the name inked in block capitals on the front of a book: SIMON DAWSON.

Carl Beeson didn't betray his interest by as much as a blink. He maintained his easy smile. 'I do apologise for butting in,' he said smoothly. 'But I must tell you that I am very interested in you, Mr. Dawson—just as I was intrigued to hear a few rumours about your brother's activities.'

'What do you mean?' Caution entered Dan Dawson's eyes.

Well, as a businessman with land interests, I hear many odd facts bandied around. It came to my notice that your brother was in Grass Valley for a special reason. He was, in fact, interested in the old tale of the treasure in the Indian Hills—but with a difference: he had documents and mining experience to back his notions.'

'Simon told no one about—'

'About the treasure?' put in Carl Beeson blandly. 'Frankly, I'm not sure who he talked to. At the time, I wasn't a bit concerned. But I'm afraid talk got around the town that he had good reason to expect to find treasure. He was seen riding out with a big man—a rough fellow—I forget his name. They went into the hills—'

'A man called Magruder. He was the one who killed poor Simon.'

'Oh, yes, that's the name. It comes back to me.' Carl Beeson set his glass and the bottle of scotch down on the table. 'Do you mind if I sit with you? And would you like to sample this whisky? It's the best.'

'If you insist,' muttered Dan Dawson.

'As your brother's next of kin, you must have his interests at heart,' continued Carl Beeson. 'You will naturally want to inquire into the tale of the treasure. And now I come to the point. You will need the help and advice of an expert on land and legal rights. For what it is worth I'd like to offer my services.'

'I have no need—' began the other man.

'I know this territory,' Beeson said. 'I've studied the history of Indian agreements, land rights, the old frontiers. I know the kind of hired help you'll need for searching through the hills. I can offer a great deal of help.'

'And what do you expect in return?' Dan Dawson was still suspicious.

'I guess expenses covered would do—unless you actually locate the treasure.' Carl Beeson laughed as if this possibility was hardly likely. He poured two drinks and set one before Dan Dawson. 'The truth is, Mr. Dawson, I find this tale of treasure in the hills quite fascinating. Perhaps lost treasure appeals to all of us. So I think a gentleman's agreement about reward for my work could suffice.' He shrugged. 'Frankly, you will need a ton of luck to retrieve the padres' loot. It's just an old tale, like so many others from the past.'

Dan Dawson's eyes narrowed behind his spectacles. 'Not quite in this instance. My

69

brother wasn't exactly a fool.'

'I'm sure he wasn't. But—'

'There is a map,' said Dan Dawson quickly, then he regretted his desire to impress.

'A map? Of the mine? The location do you mean, sir?'

'Yes. My brother copied it from sources at Casa Rio on the Mexican border.'

Carl Beeson's pink face flushed a bit with the success he was having in dealing with this man. Securing another man's confidence was an old trick with him, as more than a few had discovered to their cost in the past. He felt sure he could talk this man into accepting him as a partner. What he wanted was an hour or so with the notebooks, something he could have secured long ago with Magruder's help. But at the time, how was he to know that the big fool would mess everything up by shooting Simon Dawson in front of witnesses and then running off with the vital map?

Carl Beeson leaned over the table. The hotel was warm, the coloured waiter discreet, and the few other people in the room were out of earshot. 'A map, sir? You really have a map of the treasure location?'

Dan Dawson tapped the table angrily. 'I don't mind telling you, for I feel you are a man of integrity. There was a map showing the exact position of the old mine shaft where the padres cached the treasure. But it was stolen by

Magruder, the man who killed my brother. And possibly you know by now that he, too, is dead.'

Beeson nodded. 'Yes. I am on good terms with the sheriff, the doctor, Judge Barratt—men of that stamp. I know that the law brought this Magruder in dead. So did the lawmen retrieve the map for you?'

Dan Dawson drummed again on the table with his fingers. 'They did not. They couldn't find the map. But to me it is self-evident that that Indian girl who accompanied Magruder has my map.'

'Then the sheriff should be able to get it back for you. After all, you must be regarded as next-of-kin.'

'This girl denies having the map.'

'Surely Sheriff Thorne searched for it?'

'He looked through the saddlebags. The girl denied any knowledge of the map. I've seen the sheriff about this, but so far he hasn't acted.'

'The girl would most likely have the map on her person,' said Carl Beeson. 'She has fooled them.'

The other man nodded. 'I'm sure you're right. Damn it, I think I'll press the sheriff to take some action. In fact, I might go along to see him now, even though it's late.'

Carl Beeson pressed home his main point. 'Can I take it, Mr. Dawson, that you will allow me to work with you? This tale of buried treasure is so intriguing that I feel I must offer my services. Forget about payment or reward—initially, at any rate.' He laughed. 'If we do find the old mine shaft, you'll be an extremely wealthy man, sir.'

Dan Dawson nodded in agreement. 'Maybe I do need some help.' He smiled. 'And if you help me find the treasure my brother worked so hard to locate, you won't find me ungrateful. But first I must get that map.'

'Get Sheriff Thorne to act at once. That girl must be made to tell the truth.' Carl Beeson paused. 'I don't like to mention this, but don't trust that deputy sheriff too much. He's an ex-outlaw, pardoned by Judge Barratt and made a lawman for some crazy reason. It was a big mistake on the part of my friend the judge, I fear.'

'I'll see the sheriff now,' said Dan Dawson. He finished his whisky and felt a glow of new confidence. Sure, he needed some help. Carl Beeson, as a land expert, was just the man. And maybe he was right about that deputy; the man had shown him little respect, and where a fortune was concerned an ex-outlaw could hardly be trusted.

They shook hands before parting, as if they had made a deal, an impression Carl Beeson was careful to foster.

When Dan Dawson had left, Beeson's smiling mask was replaced by a shrewd look.

Maybe Dan Dawson could get the map back. And he was the legal owner, now that his brother was dead. If he got the map, there'd be an opportunity to copy it, seeing they were partners. And if the map didn't turn up, it was because that damn girl was hiding it. A way would have to be found to get it from her.

His cunning brain working, Carl Beeson went back to his rooms. He was sure he would win out eventually. If Dan Dawson got the map back, the rest would be easy. If the girl continued to conceal the vital piece of paper, ways would have to be found to deal with her.

★   ★   ★

Lee Baxter grinned at the tall, muscular half-breed Ute. The man smiled back. Anita seemed confident. Lee Baxter walked across the living room and looked down at Gilbert Graham. The bleeding on his face had stopped. He sat very still, obviously not a vigorous man.

Lee turned to the young man. 'So your name is Jesse Bridger. I don't know you.'

'I live in town, Deputy. I've heard of you, even if you don't know me.'

An educated voice, Lee knew at once; a Ute who'd had schooling, probably from Gilbert Graham. That figured, if the 'breed was a friend of Anita's.

Lee turned to the girl. 'I want the map.

73

Where is it?'

'How should I know?' She was smiling.

'Let's take it in order. Magruder went off with the map, figuring he could locate the treasure—and you went with him. Magruder was killed by an unknown. Prior to that you left him, taking the horse, the saddlebags and the guns. I think you found the map. He'd told you enough about it. But you pretended to be ignorant of the treasure cache. Now we have the two saloon jaspers sent after the map—by a feller we can call "Mr. X". Apparently he figures you've got that bit of paper, Anita—and so do I.'

Jesse Bridger stepped forward. 'You can't talk to Anita like that. I won't allow it.'

Lee surveyed him coldly. 'You don't have a say in this, feller.'

'He's my friend.' Anita moved closer to the half-breed and placed a hand on his arm. 'We grew up together. Jesse wants to help me—protect me. I've told him about the two men who attacked me tonight.'

Lee Baxter snapped back, 'Come off it, Anita! You know those two were after the treasure map. They didn't just attack you—they were sent here. And I figure the man who hired them is the man who shot Magruder. Do you know this man?'

'No.'

'Well, where is the map? It doesn't belong to

74

you, Anita.'

She stared back coolly. 'I haven't got this map—and I'm sick of hearing about it.'

Lee Baxter walked slowly around the room, noting the Indian rug on the pine floor, the Indian vases on the window-sill. He pointed a finger at Anita. 'I can get an order from Judge Barratt allowing me and the sheriff to search this house. Or maybe Jon Thorne will figure he's got enough authority and start poking around right away. For the last time, where's the map?'

She faced up to him, defiantly, her brown eyes glinting with anger. 'I don't know. And now get out of my father's house. You are not welcome.'

'What sort of fool game do you think you're playing?' he snapped. 'I'm certain you had that map all the time. You fooled us, Anita. Thinking back, I don't know why we believed you.'

'I'm a girl,' she mocked. 'You are gallant, Mr. Baxter.'

'Then you admit having the map?'

'I tell you, there is no map here.'

'Maybe you're right,' he growled. 'You hid it somewhere. Oh, damn the whole thing! Sheriff Thorne can take on the headache by himself. I'm going.'

Jesse Bridger was smiling broadly. His black eyes, like bits of polished stone, never left the deputy's face. Guessing at his thoughts was impossible; there was just his wide grin. And it annoyed Lee. On his way to the door, he stopped close to the half-breed.

'Where do you fit in? You haven't batted an eyelid.'

'Me no speakum English ver' good!' mocked the young man. 'No think so good. Me stupid Ute.'

Lee rasped his hand over his chin and glared. 'All right. When "Mr. X" makes another play, don't think the law'll be around to pick up the pieces. This feller will kill to get what he wants.'

Lee Baxter tramped out of the house on that sour note, feeling distinctly irritable. The day had been long and he was out of patience.

He was really annoyed with the girl. She was playing him for a fool. And if she had the map, what made her think she stood a chance of locating the lost treasure? There was a ton of work ahead of anyone who found the loot of the padres.

But maybe that was where Jesse Bridger came in. Maybe she had confided in him.

As he tramped back to his room, Lee wondered why the sight of the half-Ute put him in such a dirty mood. Was it because the fellow was so friendly with Anita? But why the hell should he worry about that?

Lee dreamed that night of a girl with a lovely

oval face—but she taunted him constantly and was not to be trusted. In the fantasy there was something odd about her—she reached out to him and then turned to a young man wearing buckskin—and that young man wanted to kill—but behind him was a menacing unknown . . .

The images faded from his brain and he slept soundly. When he awakened someone was knocking on his door. He got up and opened the door cautiously. Jon Thorne stood there, a surly expression on his face.

'All right, Mr. Baxter, I've got a job for you—when you wake up! That girl went off in the night and her pa is scared stiff. It seems she lit out with that half-breed, Jesse Bridger. And her pa is yappin' like a parrot about that map!'

CHAPTER SEVEN

ANOTHER MURDER

Carl Beeson and Dan Dawson had got together when Sheriff Jon Thorne had informed the latter about the missing girl. 'Seems like she had your map after all, Mr. Dawson,' said Thorne. 'She and that half-breed have disappeared. The girl's father tells me he heard them talking about the map...'

When the sheriff had gone back to his office, Dan Dawson hurried to Carl Beeson's premises and passed on the news.

'That girl has tricked them again! Of course, she had the map all the time. The deputy paid a visit to the house last night but was unable to get the girl to hand it over.'

'That's his yarn,' said Carl Beeson. 'I tell you, Mr. Dawson, don't trust the deputy. He's got an outlaw mentality. Maybe he's after that treasure. Sir, you could be surrounded by enemies. Now I want to help you, so here's what we'll do. We must get horses and guns and ride out after the girl.'

'But in which direction?' Dan Dawson stared. 'They could be anywhere—and the sheriff has promised to search for the girl and her companion.'

Carl Beeson gave a laugh. 'I knew you'd need someone with local knowledge, Mr. Dawson. Those two must have headed for the Indian Hills. We'll ride out and—'

'Why not leave it to the lawmen?'

'Can you afford to? Baxter is an ex-outlaw. And the sheriff is not beyond being corrupted by Baxter. Believe me, the prospect of unlimited wealth can really change people. No, I think we should ride out and see if we can track down that girl and the 'breed.'

There was one idea in Carl Beeson's mind; he wanted those notebooks that had belonged to Simon Dawson. And Dan Dawson had the notebooks. So somewhere along the line the notebooks had to leave the man's possession. Dan Dawson might have to follow his brother's fate.

Carl Beeson knew this was a game he would have to play as the cards fell. Right now it was definitely the girl who was the key—as he had guessed some time ago.

They hired horses at the livery and had the hostler fill the saddlebags. Carl Beeson brought along rifles for the saddle scabbards, but he took care not to let Dan Dawson see the derringer tucked inside his belt and covered by his coat.

Dawson eyed the rifles dubiously. 'I'm not a man of violence. I barely know how to use a Winchester.'

'This is a raw frontier,' said Carl Beeson. 'You have to protect your rights.'

Three hours later they were heading for the range of hills that had been the haunt of the Ute Indians in the past, before they had been moved to a reservation, with the exception of a few town-bred ones who were useful to the community. The wooded lands closed in on the two men as they climbed steep slopes and then slid down the shaly walls of ravines. They forded two streams and rode down a valley filled with scattered boulders. It seemed to Dan Dawson that Beeson knew his way through this territory, which was strange for a man who seemed more adapted to life behind a desk.

At the end of the day, Dan Dawson was full of doubts. He was a town man, and his riding experience had been confined to short journeys. The silent land where tall trees filled every fertile slope awed him and he thought there was no chance of finding two people in this wilderness. Even if they did find them, how could they force the girl to hand over the map? By violence? Surely that would be difficult. Threat of the law? In this huge raw land that seemed ludicrous.

But Carl Beeson was not just a desk man. At the end of the day he gestured at the ridges around them, at the land that was in part barren and supporting only cactus, and said, 'This is Indian Hills. Somewhere among these peaks and ravines is the treasure of the padres.'

'That's a fascinating thought,' said Dan Dawson. 'My brother must have been really convinced about the cache.'

'I think your brother was a clever man. A pity he allowed an obvious scoundrel like Magruder to trick him.'

'Yes. But according to the notes he made, he thought the man would be useful, with his brute strength...'

Dan Dawson looked up to the slopes of the ravine, then ahead at the numerous mountain peaks. This had been the land of the Indian, the war-like Ute who had faded from the scene, their numbers diminishing until they were placed on a reservation. This wild country had seen the mule-trains of the padres as they came north into what was unknown territory. And they had brought their amassed wealth here, believing it would eventually be shipped to Spain. None of the men who hid the treasure had survived long. Only their drawings at Casa Rio had remained.

'It seems we'll be spending some nights in this area,' remarked Dan Dawson. 'I don't relish it.'

'We'll be all right as long as it doesn't rain, but I doubt if that will happen, although rain-storms do come swiftly.'

'I can't see how we can possibly find that girl and her companion,' said the other.

'There'll be a sign—a campfire or horses' hoofmarks. And voices travel far, particularly at night. We might even sight them from a hill.'

'And then what happens?'

'We get the map.'

'But how? We are not the law. What if they defy us?'

Carl Beeson smiled. 'Don't worry, sir. We have right on our side. The map is yours. That miserable girl will hand over the map if forced.'

'She apparently has this man—this half-Ute—to help her . . .'

'An Indian,' said Carl Beeson contemptuously. 'I'll deal with him.'

'We may encounter the sheriff and his deputy.'

'They'll probably be out looking,' acknowledged the schemer.

By nightfall Carl Beeson was tired of Dawson and his critical harping on the situation. They rode on in the redness of the sinking sun, knowing they would have to make camp soon. So far they had seen no sign of the girl and her partner.

As they turned a rocky bluff they saw an old cliff face pock-marked with the round openings of ancient caves. The sandstone around the cave mouths was carved, depicting strange gargoyle faces, Indian heads, oddly shaped animals. The weather had played havoc with these memories of a cave-dwelling civilisation.

'We could camp here,' Beeson said. 'We'd be secure. We'll make a fire. There'll be room for the horses for the night—and there is grass just beyond the caves for fodder.'

'It looks gloomy,' said Dan Dawson testily.

Carl Beeson once again reflected on the idea that he could dispense with this man. All he needed was the notebooks. This carping individual was an annoyance, but a chance still existed that he could legally obtain the map. The sheriff and his deputy might chance on the girl, demand the map and get it. Then it would have to be handed over to Dawson.

Carl Beeson's better judgment prevailed. The horses were allowed to forage for grass while saddles, blankets, saddlebags, food and guns were taken into the most convenient cave. A fire was lit and the crackling red glow helped disperse some of Dawson's gloom.

They didn't realise there were other people in the narrow valley, and that their fire could be seen a long way off. A cave-mouth level with the valley bed was occupied by two persons who hadn't made a fire.

Anita Graham and Jesse Bridger sat with blankets round them. Their horses were back in the darkness of the cave, hobbled.

They had studied the map showing a rock pinnacle which was the key to locating the old mine shaft.

'There are two men down there,' muttered

Jesse Bridger. 'I'll go scout the place out and see who they are.'

'I'll come with you.'

'One can move like a shadow.'

'I have Ute blood,' she said. 'We won't be seen...'

He nodded, grinning as usual. They walked down the valley, their moccasined feet not making the slightest sound. They found cover behind large boulders, scrub and some bent old trees. Eventually they got close enough to the fire-lit cave to see the shapes of two men. Anita and Jesse paused behind a boulder big enough to conceal a horse, as a man walked to the fire and placed wood on it. As the flames leaped they were able to see the two men clearly.

'One of them is the brother of Simon Dawson,' said the girl. 'The sheriff told me about him when I rode back with him and that deputy. From their description, that's certainly Dawson.'

'The other hombre is well known in Grass Valley,' said Jesse Bridger. 'He is a land agent. He has offices in the main street and his name is Carl Beeson. I've often seen him in town.'

'They're looking for us,' said Anita. 'The man called Dawson will want the map...'

'Why is he out here with a man like Beeson? I can understand the lawmen tracking us, but this man Beeson doesn't fit in.'

'Dawson has evidently asked him for help.'

'Maybe you're right, Anita. Well, we can avoid them. We'll move like we're invisible, even in daylight. If we see them, we'll hide. They'll go around in circles. Certainly the treasure will never be found without a map...'

'I guess it'll be hard even with the map,' said the girl.

'We'll find it. Then we'll wait. Even if it takes years before we can start work on excavating, we have the patience.'

She nodded. Her eyes flashed as she shot him a glance in the dark. 'That's the difference. These men need to see gold and gems right now. They're greedy. We'll defeat them, Jesse. And with that fortune in our possession, they won't look scornfully at us again.'

He nodded, then he said thoughtfully, 'The lawmen will be in the hills, Anita...'

'Let them. We can dodge them just as we can those two. We have Ute blood in us, remember.' She paused. 'I don't like that deputy. He spoke to me so roughly. He's just like the others...'

'We could kill them and hide the bodies. They'd never be found. We have the guns to do it.' He watched her face.

Even in the darkness he saw fear in her eyes. 'Oh, no! We can't do that, Jesse! We can't kill!' As she uttered this, she wondered why she thought of Lee Baxter.

'Men have died in these hills,' Jesse said.

'Our ancestors killed without compunction...'

But she shook her head and they crept further away from the dark cliff face where the fire flared and the old Indian carvings stared down at them. She knew in that instant that she couldn't face the prospect of violence towards Lee Baxter. It was a crazy, inexplicable thought.

★   ★   ★

They were settled for the night. The fire had subsided into a heap of glowing embers at the cave mouth. They had eaten. Carl Beeson lay on his side, his back to the rock face, canvas under him and a blanket over his legs. He watched the other man read the notebooks. Carl Beeson's hat was tilted over his eyes and his deceptively youthful face betrayed no expression, which was just as well for he felt suddenly hostile towards Dan Dawson. Minutes ago he had arrived at the decision to kill the man. It was simple; Dawson had the notebooks and they were needed for a thorough search for the ancient treasure. The notebooks and the map would lead him to the fortune. The half-breed girl had the map—of that there was no doubt. He'd get it, if he had to kill her.

He had watched Dan Dawson reading the notebooks for some time. Then he had made a casual suggestion that he would be interested in learning more about this ancient tale of treasure. He had even put out a hand for the notebooks, giving his real confidence man smile. But Dan Dawson had stared suspiciously at him and had brought the notebooks close to his chest, like a man concealing a good hand of poker. At that moment, Dan Dawson signed his death warrant.

Carl Beeson feigned sleep, the blanket tucked around him. He even snored. Through narrowed eyes shaded by his hat he watched the other man settle down for the night, putting the notebooks in an inside pocket of his coat.

Beeson could have shot him with the derringer, but he had some half-formed ideas in mind. A slug in the body wouldn't fit in with his notions.

Eventually it was obvious that Dan Dawson had fallen asleep. His head sagged and his mouth was partly open. With his silly spectacles still decorating his face, he looked a fool, an irritating object that had to be abandoned. Carl Beeson got up and stood over the man, a large round rock in his hand. Dawson didn't move. The day had tired him.

Carl Beeson brought the rock down hard on the man's head. Dawson jerked but it was only a muscular reaction. Beeson slammed the rock down again. The sound of contact was ghastly in the silent cave, like the crackling of dry wood under a hefty boot. When Beeson brought the rock back again there was blood on it and his fingers were sticky and red. Dan Dawson was dead, his skull smashed. Beeson ran his bloody hand through sand. Then he took the notebooks from the man's inner pocket and looked at them. In his greed he was sure he was destined to find the old cache.

Beeson went through Dawson's pockets to make sure he had all the slips of paper, whether they might prove to be valuable or not. They were all tucked away inside the notebooks. He was careful not to disturb anything else. There was a wallet with money in it. This he left in the pocket. His plan for disposing of Dan Dawson's body called for nothing to be disturbed. He put the notebooks inside a pouch in his saddlebag. Then he dragged Dawson's body from the cave and towards a deep cleft he had noticed at the bottom of the valley.

It was hard work even for a fit man to lug a heavy body all that way and he cursed the task. But he was committed to it now. Something else struck him; he was making tracks on sandy patches. He'd have to erase them later.

He got the body to the brink of the deep cleft and then he rolled it over. He heard the corpse hit jagged rocks below. He was sure there was a cracking of bones. All the better. Later he'd present the story that Dawson had gone off alone and must have had an accident. He'd fallen from his horse and into the cleft.

Carl Beeson was well aware that the hostler in Grass Valley was a witness to the fact that the two men had ridden out together, prepared for a long ride. That couldn't be denied.

If there was an investigation, he could say that Dawson had asked him to ride with him in a search for the missing girl.

In the darkness of the valley, Carl Beeson walked back to the cave where the fire smouldered. He had the notebooks and a plausible story. He was safe. But he didn't know that two young people had been awakened by his activities. They had emerged from their cave and crept along the boulder-strewn valley to see the reason for the noises in the night. And they had seen Carl Beeson dragging the body along and pushing it into the deep cleft. Even the sound of the body crashing on the rocks came to their ears. There was no doubt in their minds that Dawson had been murdered, and Carl Beeson had killed him.

When Anita and Jesse returned to their cave at the end of the valley, they were thoughtful.

'Why did he kill him?' she asked. 'They were looking for us. Why should one kill the other?'

'It's a mystery, but we know now that Beeson has to be watched.'

When the daylight came to the rock-bound valley, they watched the further actions of the solitary man. They saw him lead a horse out to the bed of the valley and then let it wander off, fully saddled, with a rifle in the scabbard.

Then they watched Beeson ride out some time later. He disappeared along the faint natural trail that wound over the bed of the valley.

Anita and Jesse slipped into the cave the man had occupied and looked around. The fire had been scattered, and its remains buried in the sand. There was nothing to show that the cave had been used. And there was no blood, or a weapon.

'He killed the man in this cave, that's for sure.' Jesse said.

They went down to the cleft and saw the sprawled body far below. The horse had gone, looking for greener grass than the coarse brown tufts in the semi-barren valley.

'We'll move out,' said Jesse. 'And we'll look again for the pinnacle of rock shown on the map. This dead man does not concern us, Anita.'

'But we know Beeson is a killer,' she said.

He nodded soberly.

CHAPTER EIGHT

SLAIN!

Lee Baxter stared up at the rising sun and knew it would be another hot day. He and the sheriff had finished breakfast and had saddled up. They'd washed in a small pool near a spring. The sheriff was in a bad mood.

'One more day, then we ride back,' he rasped. 'No more durned time is gonna be wasted on this chore. To hell with Dawson and his map. It's probably a pipe-dream anyhow. Treasure, hell! Who says the map is genuine?'

'Simon Dawson thought it was worth spending time and money on.'

'Yeah? I've seen old maps of places I know and they don't show a true picture. And this tale of treasure is over a hundred years old.'

Lee smiled. 'Well, maybe you're right. All treasure seekers are optimists.'

'Damn the girl! Old Gilbert Graham should've given her a taste of discipline. She's too damn uppity for a part-Ute.'

'Or a part-white,' said Lee quietly.

'Now don't you start. Where'n tarnation will we find them?'

'Somewhere in the area where the treasure is supposed to be hidden.'

91

'That's real broken land with a million holes to hide in. We've already been there...'

'We'll circle back again. We might have some luck on the next circuit.'

'I'd like to know where they camped for the night,' mumbled the sheriff. 'That gal sure goes for her own kind. Jesse Bridger was taught by Gilbert Graham in town. Too damned much education, I figure. Was even given a job by Herb Parsons as a clerk in the bank. Did you ever hear of an Injun working in a bank! And now look—he rides off with that girl. Sleeping together, I have no doubt...'

'You can't say that,' snapped Lee.

'Jon Thorne shot him a hard look. 'But I do say it. She went off with Magruder, too.'

'She wouldn't let Magruder touch her. It'll be the same with Bridger.'

'Is that what you figure? I say they're two of a kind.'

Lee Baxter scowled, wishing the sheriff would shut up. He didn't want to believe anything bad about the girl, but he admitted he disliked the idea that she was associating with Jesse Bridger. From his own experience he knew that if you gave a dog a bad name, it would stick. Anita was being foolish; she had no right to the map. It was the property of Dan Dawson. Something had gotten into the girl.

After about an hour, when the sun was warming the numerous ravines in this jagged

92

land, they climbed a knoll of shale and sand and sat their horses for some time, watching the natural trails. Lee Baxter had a spy-glass and was using it when he saw the movement of a horse. He stared and then handed the glass over to the sheriff.

'Down there—among the scrub bush—past the thorn—in that little pass between the bluffs. A riderless horse.'

The sheriff took the glass and looked for some moments. You're right. Let's go down. Might be a lead.'

They jigged their animals down the slope, the horses' haunches sliding nearly to the ground. They reached level land and rode to the narrow defile that led over to the bluffs.

It took all of ten minutes of riding, picking a way through rocks and avoiding thorn clumps, then they came to the riderless horse. The animal stood, ears pricked. Lee reached out and grabbed the reins. He scrutinised the saddle and the bag hanging from the pommel. He saw a brand mark on the horse's flank.

'That brand mean anything to you, Sheriff?' he asked. 'You've been a Grass Valley man longer than me.'

'It's from the big livery in town,' Thorne said.

'A hired mount?'

'I think so. Now where's the rider. He's left a good rifle in that scabbard.'

'And some grub in the saddlebags,' said Lee. He had slipped the buckle and stared into a bag. Now he brought out two cans of beans. 'Let's mosey around, Sheriff. Maybe the rider was thrown, or maybe the horse wandered off and he's searching for it.'

'Some feller from Grass Valley,' mused the sheriff. 'Now who'd be up in these hills? It don't look like a prospector's horse—no gear. And it don't belong to the girl or Bridger—not a hired mount.'

They took the animal in tow and searched the broken terrain, moving slowly through the seemingly endless clefts. They were looking for the girl and also keeping a sharp lookout for a man on foot. Twice they had to back-track, finding themselves in dead-end ravines.

After some hours of this, the sun hitting hard on their backs, they cut back, turning in a wide loop. If they went too far north they would be moving away from the area where they hoped to spot Anita Graham and Jesse Bridger.

As they reached a stretch of level ground, a little valley with a sandy bed studded with cholla now in yellow bloom, they saw a man riding ahead. He was on a slow-moving animal, his hat pulled low.

'Now who is that hombre?' Lee asked. 'A man in a fine suit up in these ravines? The thorns will tear it to hell...'

Jon Thorne stared. For a man approaching

middle-age, he had good sight. He said, 'That's Carl Beeson, the land agent in Grass Valley. Now what in thunder is he doin' out here?'

'Who is Beeson?'

'He has an office in town—deals in property and land. Smooth feller. A charmer, what with his silver hair and pink face and big smile. But then, ain't all speculators real smooth?'

In no great rush, for the other man had seen them, Lee and the sheriff rode along the valley floor, bringing the lost horse with them.

Carl Beeson smiled. 'Howdy, men! Say, that's Mr. Dawson's horse! Where'd you find it? Where is he?'

'Dawson? Dan Dawson?' Concern glinted in the sheriff's eyes.

'We rode out together,' said Carl Beeson. 'He asked me to help him. He wanted to locate that 'breed girl who has his map.'

'You know about the map?'

'Sure. He told me about it.' Beeson pushed back his hat, revealing his thick silver hair. 'I can't say that I considered his notions about this lost treasure to be very reliable, but when he asked me to ride out with him, I agreed. But he went off last night—alone—saying he'd take a final look around before turning in for the night. He didn't come back, Sheriff. I looked around, but darkness had fallen.'

'Where was this?'

'In a grassy little hollow some miles away. I

doubt if I could even find it again. Look, that is Dan Dawson's horse. Where'd you find it?'

Lee gestured to the peaks behind them. 'Way back. Why didn't Dawson leave the search for the girl to us?'

'I guess he thought we'd be additional hands in the search for this girl and the map,' explained Carl Beeson. He sighed. 'I'm worried about Dawson. What do you think could have happened?'

'He either fell from his horse or it was badly tethered and wandered off,' said Lee.

Carl Beeson looked grave. 'I don't like it. I should have persuaded Mr. Dawson to stay in town.'

Lee glared. 'But you didn't. You rode out—with rifles, I see. And Dawson was no gunhand. So where did he get the Winchester? And what the hell did you figure to do if and when you did meet up with the girl? Threaten her? Let me tell you that Jesse Bridger is armed.'

Carl Beeson didn't lose his smile. 'You merely confirm my doubts about this whole thing, Deputy. Perhaps I should ride back to Grass Valley.'

'Ain't you gonna stick around and look for Dawson?'

'Well, I'll do that as I move through these hills. In fact, I'll take his horse along with me in case I find him. But I tell you, gentlemen, all

96

this just makes me more doubtful. Dawson could wander around lost in this land for days. It's terrible country—I'll be glad to go back. This whole notion of a map and treasure is crazy, anyway.'

The sheriff nodded as if agreeing. 'I'm plumb tired of the whole thing, too. All that concerns me is the murder of Simon Dawson—and the man who killed him is dead.'

'There was also a tubby little hombre called Pete who got himself killed,' Lee reminded Thorne. 'And it wasn't an accident.'

'All right,' grumbled Jon Thorne. 'I'll talk to the skinny feller we've got in the hoosegow and maybe get a lead. I tell you, Baxter, I'll stick around here for another day, and if we don't catch up with this girl then the map can go to blazes.'

A little later they parted company with Beeson. The man rode off in an easterly direction, taking Dawson's horse on a lead rope. Lee and Thorne watched him go and when Lee turned thoughtfully in his saddle, he said:

'Rifles . . . Two town gents with Winchesters. And now one has got himself lost. Kind of queer . . .'

The sheriff and Lee Baxter rode on through the maze of narrow defiles that made this terrain look like it had been fashioned by some demented act of creation. They were taking a wide loop again, looking along veritable slots in the rock. A hundred men could hide in such a jumble. And a horse could be led into a cleft where overhanging thornbush would conceal it like a curtain. Jon Thorne was emphatic that this was the legendary area of the La Mina Del Padres. Pinnacles of rock stabbed into the sky.

'A lost mine shaft in this goddamn land,' mused Lee Baxter. 'After a hundred and twenty years, finding it will be like picking up a needle in a haystack after an all-night drunken binge.'

The sheriff mopped his brow. 'Gosh almighty, I've had enough. Damn the map! That girl can stick around here for the rest of her life—and that fool Bridger with her. I reckon we'll take these horses back before we lame 'em.'

'And Dawson?'

'He can take his chances!' barked Thorne. 'I tell you—gold drives men loco. Simon Dawson is dead—and so is Magruder. I hope there ain't gonna be any more. It sure won't be me.'

Lee nodded as if in assent. But he wasn't totally with the sheriff. 'You can ride back,' he said. 'I'll give it another day or so. Somebody has to find Anita and talk sense to her.'

The mention of her name seemed to be a signal. From about half a mile away, as near as they could judge, deep among the jagged rocks that lay as if a giant hand had fashioned them, came a shot. The sharp crack of sound seemed

98

to hang in the air.

Lee stared into the distance, listening intently. 'That was a rifle.'

Jon Thorne jabbed heels to his horse. 'All right, let's go!'

The rough land was against speed. They made the animals respond to heel jabbing but the route was tortuous. Then they were on a stretch of arid land and they went over it at a trot. Finally they had to haul in the horses because they were baffled. They stood in their stirrups and looked up at the layers of slab rock that rose on all sides. There was no sign of movement and no more shots. The rock rolled like flat ledges to a cliff about two hundred yards back. This vertical face was of red stone and ran for a good distance. Here and there, holes in the cliff looked like cave mouths but as Lee Baxter stared he realised they were old mine shafts. He pointed, speaking to Jon Thorne.

'See them? Old workings, huh?'

The sheriff nodded. 'Yeah, men have been poking around here for sign of gold quartz for ages.'

'Long ago, you mean. The padres apparently found a mine one hundred and twenty years ago and cached their loot in it.'

'Yeah. They sure picked on some wild country.'

Lee urged his horse along the sandy bed.

'Now who the blazes fired that shot? What was it all about?'

'We're lookin' for a girl and a young feller,' said the sheriff grimly. 'When we find 'em, we might get some answers. I doubt if there's anyone else in this country.'

'Have you forgotten Beeson?' asked Lee.

'He rode off in the other direction.'

'In this country he could double back and we'd have no more chance of seeing him than of seeing a yellow lizard on a yellow rock. And there's also Dawson.'

'He lost his horse.'

Lee nodded. 'You win that one, Sheriff.'

At that moment Lee's keen ears caught a low, moaning sound. It drifted from the folds of slab rock like a ghostly voice crying out. Lee wheeled his horse around and rode slowly along the rim of the rock. Then he dismounted.

'Did you hear that, Sheriff?'

'Well, I heard something. Could be the wind . . .'

Lee Baxter climbed the rock and went carefully forward, his Colt in his hand. Then the sound reached him again. The moan carried a message of pain and an attempt to communicate. Abandoning caution, Lee ran forward. Behind him Thorne came on foot. The two horses stayed put.

Lee had to search the hollows in the folds of rock until he located the source of the moaning.

100

Then, when he looked down at the body his eyes narrowed and became bitter.

'Over here, Sheriff,' he snarled.

Jon Thorne came running. 'Jesse Bridger!'

Lee raised the young man's head. The red stain over the heart told all.

'Who was it, Jesse?' Lee asked. 'What happened? Where's Anita?'

The young fellow opened his eyes and tried to grin. But pain shuddered through him. He opened his mouth but the only sound was an incoherent moan. He tried to form words but they wouldn't come. His lips moved but only blood and saliva trickled out.

Then he died in Lee's arms. Lee tore at the shirt and grimaced when he saw the terrible wound.

'He's gone, Baxter,' mumbled the sheriff.

Lee eased the body gently back. 'There's a man called Beeson in these hills—and he had a rifle. I reckon that town gent can use a gun. But I want to know what's happened to Anita Graham.'

CHAPTER NINE

THE TORTURER

'You expect me to believe that tale?' Carl Beeson said.

Two horses stood in the narrow slot of rock; one was the mount hired by the land speculator, and the other was Anita's. The concealment offered by the deep, rectangular fissure in the slab rock was perfect, with overhanging scrub forming a roof to the hideout. The animals were at the far end. The mouth of the slot looked out into a sandy coulee filled with bunch grass.

'I haven't got the map,' Anita flung at him.

'You're a damned lying bitch!' Anger flushed through every nerve of his body. She had denied having the map right from the moment he'd got the drop on her and walked up with his rifle to the crevice where Jesse Bridger lay dying. She had tried to grab at the half-breed's gun but he had kicked it away.

He'd spotted them first. They had been leading their horses through a defile, moving slowly, pointing to rocky peaks nearby and talking. They hadn't noticed him even when he had stood up, taking careful aim with the Winchester, and had fired at the young man. Then it had been too late. The man had staggered back under the impact of the bullet and the girl had had to support him. They had tottered to the crevice in the rock and, when Carl Beeson leaped over, rifle ready, the girl had been too slow in trying to obtain Jesse Bridger's gun.

He had been tempted to kill her and had nearly done just that until she screamed at him that she didn't have the map.

'We've hidden it!' she had raged.

So at rifle point he had forced her to leave the dying young man and go to her horse. The other animal had wandered off. They had moved on, with some urgency, Beeson just behind her. After some thirty minutes of grim searching he'd found this slot in the rock. He had to stop and deal with her.

'You're lying,' he said through clenched teeth.

'I'm not,' she said. 'We hid it.'

'Why should you? Give me one good reason why you should hide that damned map.'

'We knew men were after us.'

'You mean the lawmen?'

'Not just them. We knew they'd ride after us. But you, too.'

He held the rifle waist high. 'You lying little slut, you didn't know a thing about me.'

'We saw you with the man called Dawson, at the Indian caves.'

He tensed. 'Where were you?'

103

'In a cave, just as you were with that other man. And then you killed him. You threw the body into a cleft in the rock.' She glared at him. 'I know you for a killer, Mr. Beeson. And if Jesse dies—'

'He'll die,' said Carl Beeson. 'But that's not important. I want that map.'

'Why did you kill Dawson?' Instinct told her to stall him, delay him.

His face was set coldly. With his silver hair falling down the nape of his neck he looked a distinguished gentleman, even with his suit now torn with thorn and covered with dust.

'You might as well know,' he said. 'It might make you hand over that map—because I don't believe you hid it. I killed Dawson because he had some notebooks that supplement the map.'

'I think you also shot Mick Magruder,' she said. 'Am I right?'

'Yes.' Cold now, his anger replaced by determination, he put out a hand. 'Give me that map. I'm sure you've got it on you. You didn't hide it. And I looked through the pockets of the 'breed before we left—he didn't have it.'

'It's hidden and you won't find it.'

'You'll die, you damned Ute!'

'Then you'll *never* find the map,' she mocked. 'The secret will die with me.' She studied him carefully. 'I think you sent those two men to my father's house. They asked for the map. Then one was killed—to stop him talking, I guess.

And if you killed Mick Magruder it's because you knew—or thought you knew—that he had this valuable piece of paper.'

He regarded her with glinting eyes. 'You seem determined to piece it together. Yes, I knew Magruder. I encouraged him to work with Simon Dawson, but I didn't expect him to kill the man so stupidly and thereby bring the law into this. I had to shut his mouth. Now let's quit talking. Hand over the map. You don't fool me. You didn't hide that map.'

'But we did. And if you kill me, it will stay hidden.'

He slapped the rifle butt. 'I can make you talk. I'll start shooting at you if you don't talk or produce the map—and the first slug will be in your thigh. Then the other thigh. And after that a bullet will shatter your ankle. You'll never walk again...'

'The shots will be heard in these hills for miles around,' she countered swiftly. 'Have you thought of that?'

'Those two lawmen will be a long way off.'

'Then you've seen them!' She backed to the rock wall. 'You're not in such a good position, Mr. Killer Beeson.'

Seething hatred for this girl assailed him, but it didn't cloud his judgment. He knew shots might be heard—and traced.

He swiftly reversed his hold on the rifle and swung the butt at the side of her head. It was a carefully placed blow, designed to hurt and frighten but not to knock her unconscious. Even so she cried out with the pain and retreated from him, pressing against the rock wall. He crowded in and hit her again. Dazed, she sank to the ground. He leaned over her and relentlessly probed into every pocket of her buckskin dress. Then, finding nothing that even resembled the piece of paper, he tore at the thongs that fastened the neck of the dress. She tried to push him away, crying, dazed. He hit her this time with his fist. Gone was the image of the desk man, the polite man of business. He pulled down the neck of the dress and, as the girl lay there with swimming senses, he searched inside her bodice for the missing map.

As the girl lay there in a daze, he ran his hands over her, searching her down to her moccasins. Then he stood up, breathing hard with annoyance. The map was not on her. Holding the rifle, he went back to his horse and searched the saddlebags without success. In the end, he waited for the girl to recover her senses and then he grabbed her and shook her violently.

'Where did you hide that map? You'll tell me, by God!'

Anita huddled on the ground, trying to fasten the thongs at the neck of her dress while she glared her hatred at this man. Even with her faculties dulled from the blows she'd received, she had felt his hands running over her body.

Breathing hard, he raised his hand to strike her again. 'I wish I could kill you—get rid of you—but I need that map. The notebooks aren't enough. You'll talk. I have a knife in my saddlebags. You, as part Indian, should know how much torture can be inflicted with a knife.'

She laughed at him, a harsh sound full of contempt. 'I won't talk. You can kill me, but you'll never get that map.'

He walked the length of the rock-bound slot, thinking swiftly, trying to control his implacable fury. He stared carefully around the corner of the rock. The silent land shimmered in the bright sunlight, giving no answers to his problem. One thing he had to bear in mind was the fact that the two lawmen were somewhere out there.

He returned to the girl. 'We'll hole up here. We'll spend the rest of the day in hiding. I have plenty of patience. You'll eventually tell me where to pick up that map. I think the lawmen will give up and ride away.'

Carl Beeson spent the next hour watching the girl, tormenting her with threats and references to the dead Jesse Bridger. She huddled in the rocky prison, her face blank. She was recovering from the blows he had handed out to her, but she feared the next round of torture. Could she withstand savage treatment with a knife? And was it worth the punishment? The quest for the lost mine shaft had cost Jesse his life, and she felt she was to blame for it. She had persuaded Jesse to help her. She'd known the way he had felt about her. And now he was dead.

Thinking about Jesse only weakened her resolve. Suddenly the prospect of treasure, even the thought of getting even with all the people who had sneered at her for being part-Ute seemed futile. Her notions had cost Jesse his life; she was to blame. She had no excuse; she had no legal claim to the map. It had belonged to Simon Dawson and then presumably to his brother—and both were dead.

Carl Beeson's patience was not as limitless as he had stated. He came closer to the girl, his pink face working with resentment. He had the knife in his hand, having taken it from his saddlebag.

'We're wasting time. You will talk now. The badgetoters will be far away. They can't track shots; echoes leave nothing behind. They will give up. I think the sheriff particularly has lost interest. So you will talk...'

He lunged with the knife. The shining blade slashed close to her face, missing by an inch. Carl Beeson laughed. 'That's just to scare you. I'll get nearer to your face each time. Do you want to look like a scarred warrior of the Utes, or are you sufficiently white to appreciate good

108

looks?'

'You are more of a savage than any brave from the reservation,' she said.

'Damn you—talk!' he shouted. 'Where's the map?' And he swiped the blade close to her cheek.

Only by her flinching back had the blade missed drawing blood. She tried to get away from him but then her back was against the wall.

He tried a slightly different tactic. He ran the blade down her buckskin-clad arm. The buckskin parted under the keen edge and blood showed. She gasped and pressed back. He ran the blade down her other arm.

'Are you a fool?' he sneered. 'Just tell me where you hid that map. Then I'll let you go.'

'You'll kill me,' she shouted. 'I can testify against you. I know you killed Dan Dawson—and where you put the body. You'll never let me go free to talk about you.'

'Clever girl. But you'll talk ... when I start working on your face.'

A change of expression darted across her face. 'If I do tell you ... will you let me go now?'

'Don't try to fool me,' he said. 'I know what you're thinking. The answer is, you'll accompany me to wherever you've hidden that map. And if it's not there you'll suffer.'

There was only one way out—to catch him by

surprise. He thought she was terror-stricken and helpless. He was smiling now. His confidence was such that he had put the rifle to one side. She knew she couldn't beat him to that weapon. Even if she got her hands on it, she wouldn't be able to level it quickly enough.

She waited until he began to make another move with the knife. At that moment he expected her to shrink back. But she leaped to one side with all the superhuman effort only a desperate person can summon. Taken by surprise, his reaction was slow and her leap landed her on all fours. He twisted and tried to hack at her with the knife. The blade hissed through the air and dug into the earth. Then Anita ran with frantic speed.

In seconds she was at the opening in the rock-bound slot. She went through it, her arms streaked with blood, her face showing dark bruises. She knew she had only this one chance of getting free.

Carl Beeson wasn't really slow in his chase, but she had terror to thrust her on. He jumped forward and then cursed, knowing that he needed the rifle. He leaped back and grabbed at the weapon. He had his hidden derringer, but it wasn't much use except at very close range.

Getting the rifle had cost him precious seconds. When he ran out of the slot, Anita's bobbing head was some distance away. He shouldered the gun and cursed when he realised the two badgetoters might still be within hearing distance.

He ran down a coulee, but she had disappeared. He began climbing a series of layered slabs of rock. When he got to the top of this vantage point he stared around for a sign of the girl. But she had gone, vanishing among the endless holes and clefts.

He went on, glancing to right and left. His face was set, his eyes glinting. An observer from Grass Valley who knew this man would have been astonished to see the transformation from a smooth townsman to a crazed killer.

CHAPTER TEN

TRIP TO CHINESE CAMP

The two lawmen found her a few hours after leaving Jesse Bridger's body in the crevice. She was running erratically. They saw her stagger and then lean against a boulder. Wasting no time, they rode her down.

'Anita! What's happened to you?' Lee Baxter slid from the saddle and saw the blood on her arms, the bruises on her face. He placed an arm around her shoulder and steadied her. 'Where's your horse? Where've you been?'

The feel of his arm around her was reassuring, and for a long moment she stared into his eyes. Then she muttered, 'Jesse? He's been shot...'

'We found him,' said Lee. 'He's dead. Then we spotted his horse in the distance...'

'Well, we figured it was his horse,' put in the sheriff. He sent an appraising glance at the girl. 'All right, who was it? Beeson?'

'He shot Jesse,' cried the girl. 'He drygulched us ... I—I couldn't do anything to stop him...'

'Another one after that map!' raged Thorne. 'And you, girl—you've tricked us all the way. You've got no right to hold onto that scrap of

112 of112

paper, so hand it over. And I mean now.'

'I haven't got it,' was her reply.

The senior lawman lost his temper. 'You're lyin'! Come on, where is it?'

Lee said, 'Hold it, Sheriff. Let's see if we can bandage her arms first.'

Jon Thorne glared at him. 'Now look, Baxter, I want an end to this business—and possession of the map might just do that.'

'It's hidden,' Anita said. 'Beeson wanted it, now you. I don't trust you, even if you are lawmen . . .'

'Does that include me?' Lee asked.

'Maybe. You're an ex-outlaw.' She backed away from him, her eyes gleaming defiantly. 'What would you do if you thought you could find a fortune worth millions of dollars? You broke the law for stupid sums of money in the past, so are you immune to temptation?'

Sheriff Jon Thorne got down from his mount and approached the girl, wagging a stern finger. 'Now look here, we're the law.'

She smiled coldly. 'Have you no greed? Doesn't the thought of a cache of gold, silver and gems excite you?'

The older man made an angry sound. 'I'm right out of patience with you, Miss Graham—or should I call you Rising Sun or some other damn Ute name!'

'I am more white than Ute!' she screamed, all the terror of the past few hours going into her fury. 'Even if I were wholly Indian I'd have as much right to dignity as any woman in Grass Valley.'

Jon Thorne grabbed her shoulders. 'You've got that map! Where is it? Hand it over!'

She threw a look of scorn back at him. 'I've told you, just as I told Beeson—it's hidden. And maybe I won't tell anyone where to find it. Maybe I'll keep the secret to myself...'

Lee tried to mollify her. 'Look, Anita, the ownership of this document will have to be settled. Maybe the state will place a claim on such a vast treasure if it is found.' He held her gaze earnestly. 'It doesn't belong to you. Simon Dawson did all the research, and he's dead...'

She nearly weakened as he held her hand. Her gaze dropped. She struggled to maintain her defiance and to this end she threw words at them. 'That dirty killer—Beeson—murdered Dan Dawson. Jesse and I saw him dump the body in a rocky cleft just beside the Indian caves. He also killed Mick Magruder—to shut him up, he said. And he shot that tubby little man who broke into my father's house—to keep him quiet.'

'Beeson, huh?' growled the sheriff. 'Maybe we should look for him. We can't let a killer wander around free.'

'You should go home, Anita,' Lee said. 'Your father is worried about you.'

She nodded. 'I haven't been a good daughter

114

to him. First I ran off with Mick Magruder and now it's my fault that Jesse Bridger is dead.'

'Then you'll tell us where to pick up that map? And you'll go home?'

Her eyes flashed. 'I'll go home, but I'll keep the secret of the map's hiding place.'

'Why? What can you do about it? You'll be watched. The news would get around about the map and your life would be in danger.'

'I'll bargain,' she said. 'I'll make a deal for the Ute nation.'

Jon Thorne had no more patience. 'You *are* goin' back to town all right, girlie—to jail.'

'Jail?'

'You're keeping somethin' that doesn't lawfully belong to you,' barked the lawman. 'You'll stay in the hoosegow while Judge Barratt makes a decision on this crazy business.'

They had things to do before they could ride off. The girl's slashed arms were washed in a spring, then bandaged with a clean bandanna from the sheriff's saddlebag. It was then that they wished they had another horse. They had lost the wandering animal which had belonged to Jesse Bridger, and the girl's mount was still with Carl Beeson. The townsman would undoubtedly be very cautious now that he had lost the girl and had probably left the hills or was in hiding.

'So it's Beeson,' Lee said when they were finally ready. 'He's "Mr. X", the man Simon

115

Dawson referred to as someone Magruder knew. It all figures.'

As they had made ready for the ride back, the girl had told them a bit more. 'Carl Beeson is mad. The thought of all that wealth has turned his head. He was going to kill me the moment he had that map . . .'

But she refused to tell where the map was hidden. All she would say was, 'Jesse and I thought it best to hide the map. We knew you were in the hills—and we'd seen Beeson kill his partner. We thought we could memorise the main details, including the pinnacle of rock that is the key to the location of the old mine.'

Anita preferred to ride with Lee Baxter. His bedroll was tied on the sheriff's mount to make room for her. As they plodded through the hot land, she was still defiant.

Turning in the saddle, Lee said, 'Give this silly plan up, Anita. It won't work. You can't find the padres' loot.'

'*You*, too?' she said. 'You think I'm of no consequence?'

'I didn't say that.'

'I'm just a fool girl—is that it? Part-Ute, neither white nor Indian.'

'Sheriff Thorne will put you in jail,' he warned. 'He's a stubborn galoot—and the judge will back him up. Where do you go from there?'

'They can't keep me in jail forever.'

'Damn it, you've got too much nerve for a

girl! It won't work, I tell you. You've got no right to that map.'

'Did Simon Dawson have any right?' she countered. 'He found the map among some ancient documents. It didn't belong to him. Who does own a treasure trove? Maybe it belongs to the finder—and I might be the one.'

He dragged in his breath and said harshly, 'Don't forget Beeson. He's around and he's a killer.'

That night in Grass Valley, true to his word, Sheriff Thorne locked the girl in the jail and allowed only her father to see her. The indignity of it all only made Anita harden her resolve. 'You will never get the map!' she shouted furiously at them. 'Never! It will rot where it's hidden—unless I'm accepted as a person with some right to it.'

Her father tried to plead with her, but she was in no mood to listen to him. Old and ineffectual, he couldn't cope with her anger. He went away shaking his head, sad to hear of the death of Jesse Bridger, a boy he had taught and encouraged for many years.

Carl Beeson's name was on the wanted list. When Judge Barratt gave approval, a wanted poster would be printed. Jon Thorne's last act that night was to go along to Beeson's premises in the main stem and look through the office. He found some papers concerning land deals, but that was all.

A man with two horses, a derringer and a rifle came down out of the Indian Hills just before darkness fell. But he didn't make for Grass Valley. That town was now closed to him, he realised. He'd had plenty of time to think as his horse covered the miles. With hunches that were strangely correct, he felt sure that the girl had reached safety. One possibility was that she had been picked up by the lawmen. They were out there to find her and they were competent men. Even if they missed her, she was strong enough to wander on until she came out of the hills and encountered someone to whom she could appeal for help. His hunches told him she'd reached Grass Valley.

Carl Beeson rode west of the town, an idea forming in his mind. He knew how to reach Chinese Camp, a run-down settlement where the remnants of the Chinese railroad gangs had settled after the Union Pacific Railroad had been completed in that area and the surplus labour dispensed with. The ramshackle scattering of shacks lay on a desolate plain some twenty-five miles west of Grass Valley. There was no law here because the Chinese gave no trouble and were a self-contained community living a frugal life. They grew rice in swampland that lay in a hollow, a freakish thing in this otherwise dry land. They kept goats and sheep, and some of the men travelled long distances to work for ranchers and miners, always returning to their womenfolk, sometimes after an absence of weeks. Chinese Camp was never a white man's settlement; life there was too hard for even the lowest range bum.

But, strangely, Carl Beeson knew one man there who could help him; a man he had assisted a year ago with a land deal in Poker Canyon. That land had belonged to Yip Tee, a small round little Chinaman who had saved money with a desperation unknown to whites, and had then bought the ground. A miner had wanted it, convinced there was gold on it. He bought it from Yip Tee, with Carl Beeson's help, but there wasn't any gold. By the time this was known, Yip Tee had his money and had retired to Chinese Camp. Carl Beeson had pocketed his not inconsiderable commission—and made a friend. This amused him. The deal had been relatively small, a run-of-the-mill transaction. Beeson had been back to Chinese Camp once before, wondering if there was any value in this flat, dreary land. He knew the trail, which was just as well for he completed half the distance that night in the dark before resting, too tired to go on.

When he rode into Chinese Camp early the next day he was observed but ignored, for the slant-eyed men of that community minded their own business. Yip Tee was not hard to find. He was forty but looked a great deal older, his hairless face lined like that of a monkey. He had his own shack. Others might live two and three to a cabin, but Yip Tee as a man of capital, lived alone, employing others to do his hard work and hiring out his own countrymen for fees as he dreamed of his extraordinary years as a young man in China, before being lured to this cursed land. Yip Tee had been occupied in an unusual job in those days.

Carl Beeson knew all about him; they'd talked at length when they'd done business together. Yip Tee, like many orientals, was full of gratitude when a man did him a favour.

Smiling, he came to his shack door when Carl Beeson rode through the settlement. Weary with the muscle-stretching exercises of the past two days, Beeson got down from the saddle. He looped the reins of the two horses to a post outside the shack. Before he had finished this chore, Yip Tee was babbling smoothly in his reasonably good English:

'Ah, my good frien', you do me honour. You visit this humble man. Please to enter . . . we will drink some wine.'

'Wine will be fine,' said Carl Beeson through dry, cracked lips. 'God it's getting hot already. But Yip Tee, my friend, I am glad to see you.'

This was no exaggeration, for already

120

Beeson's cunning mind could see the possibilities in the art of this exile from China. But his visit must seem to be inspired by friendship, highly valued by the oriental.

Later, when they were seated on straw mattresses on the floor and drinking wine from china bowls, the talk got around to Beeson's reason for the visit. Yip Tee was curious, although his smiling face did not show it. He sat and grinned, his smock hiding his round frame, a straw hat flopping on his head. 'It is, ah, a long ride from Grass Valley. And two saddled horses—you have had a frien'—what you, ah, call a podner, so?'

'I need your help, Yip Tee.'

The other bowed. 'I am your humble frien'.'

'And I am yours too, Yip Tee.'

'We are men who help each other,' said the Chinaman.

'And you can always count on me,' said Carl Beeson graciously. He took off his hat. 'What do you see, my friend? A man with silver hair—is that not so? Now I know you can change not only the colour of a man's hair, but you can alter his facial appearance...'

Yip Tee grinned and nodded. 'It is long time since I do this kind of work ...' he began.

'But you have all the materials at hand. That's something you told me the last time we met. I was really interested in your art...'

'It is something I will never lose.'

'You were a valuable man in the Chinese theatre, a makeup artist, I think we in the West might call you.'

'The theatre in China called for devils and saints,' said Yip Tee, his black eyes bright with new interest. 'Every face is painted. An actor does not show his real face, and I was the man who gave them new faces ... sometimes thick with paint ... or maybe just a leetle change ... a line above the jaw or around the eyes. Also, my frien', I can make your face thinner or fatter...'

Carl Beeson smiled and raised his bowl of wine. 'I want only changes in my face that can stand up in the light of day. Let me tell you a story, Yip Tee. I want to visit Grass Valley and move around so that nobody will recognise me. It is a joke, you see.'

'A joke? Ah, yes, the American funny joke. We Chinese do not know how to joke, but I can make you a new face and dye your hair any colour, my frien'. And if you change your clothes, your own people will not know you.'

'What do you suggest?'

The other's grin was positively painful. 'Why not go as a Chinaman? I tell it to you, my frien'—Yip Tee can make you into real Chinese man ver' fast, and you will never get second look from anybody.'

Carl Beeson slapped the palm of his hand against his knee. 'By God, that's the answer. I'll be able to move around Grass Valley without any trouble and I'll locate that damned girl and deal with her ...' His thoughts ran on, his words slurring to nothing.

The work on the disguise didn't begin for some time. Yip Tee was not a man to be hurried, and the cordialities had to be preserved. In any case, Carl Beeson planned to ride back to Grass Valley in the early hours of the next morning, after some rest.

His mind was never free from the fantasy of the limitless wealth that lay hidden in the terrible Indian Hills. He could buy a vast rancho over the Mexican border, live like a king and become a power in the land. Or life in the East could be explored. A great mansion, land, the best in clothes and possessions could be his. There was no limit to what he could do.

And it was there, buried behind a wall of clay, placed there all those years ago by the labours of a team of padres and their followers; a fortune that was never brought to light because of the deaths of those who knew the secret.

And a slip of a girl held the key to this wealth. She had hidden the map somewhere; had she told the law about it?

When Carl Beeson left Chinese Camp the next day, he had exchanged not only his clothes, but his horse. He rode an old sway-backed mare that could walk all day but couldn't raise a gallop. His suit had been discarded for the smock of a Chinaman, and a coolie hat sat on his black hair. He had wooden sandals on his feet. His face was yellowed and lined. Gone was the healthy pink colour. The saddle and gear on his horse was ancient and worthless by any standards. He had only to keep his mouth shut and he would pass for one of the despised Chinese. The makeup on his face was weather-proof and would improve with travel dust. He was Chou Sing.

But beneath his shapeless clothes he carried the derringer.

CHAPTER ELEVEN

APPOINTED GUARDIAN

'You're a fool, Anita! You're on the wrong side of the law.'

He stared at her, wondering at the rebellious streak in this lovely girl. Was it a chip on her shoulder, created during the years in which she had grown up in Grass Valley, knowing she had Indian blood? Or was she being defiant just to show the law and anyone who backed it that she was not with them? She lightly gripped the iron bars of the cell and looked out at him mockingly.

She said, 'Well, *you* should know something about being on the wrong side of the law. Tell me, did you ever go to jail?'

Lee Baxter held his temper in check and said, 'I earned a pardon, and I can tell you I'm glad. But you're just being obstinate, Anita. That map has got to be found and then put in safe-keeping until the law decides who can lay claim to it. For all we know, Dan Dawson might have relatives.'

'I'll tell you one thing, Lee Baxter. You'll never find the map without my help.' She tried to shake the bars. Down the passage, near the door leading to the sheriff's office, Jon Thorne

125

stood, shaking his head dubiously. 'When are you going to let me out?' she cried.

'We're going to see Judge Barratt today,' Lee said. 'I reckon something will be done. It ain't right for a girl to be in jail.' Lee glanced at the cell three blocks down the passage. The tall fellow with the long nose, the man he'd got the drop on in Gilbert Graham's house, was still inhabiting the square space. Judge Barratt had decreed that the man stay in jail indefinitely. 'A girl shouldn't be kept here with dirty range tramps,' Lee said. 'Still, you've only got yourself to blame, Anita.'

'Why aren't you out searching for Carl Beeson?' she demanded. 'He's a killer. Jesse would be alive today if it wasn't for Beeson.'

'We're only two men,' Lee said. 'There's a lot of land out there. But maybe we'll get a lead on the skunk.'

The sheriff called gruffly from the end of the passage. 'Come on, Baxter, you're wastin' your time with that little bitch.'

Anita screamed at him, 'You treat me with respect! I shall complain to the judge about your treatment of me.'

As Thorne turned away, he muttered, 'He ain't too fond of Utes, girl. He was made a widower by Injuns—and he ain't never forgot it.'

The appointment to see Judge Barratt was for later in the day, so there was no alternative but

126

for Anita to cool off. She watched Lee Baxter go, furious with herself and not able to understand the confusion in her mind. She felt obliged to flare up at this lean, grave-faced deputy whenever they met, and when he departed she felt the same strange regrets. There was something about him that she liked; yet there was also this compulsion to defy him.

She had spent one night in the cell, knowing that Lee Baxter had protested on her behalf. She'd heard him yell at the sheriff. 'And what happens if you have to shove some drunken foul-mouth in this jail? Does she have to listen to that?'

But Jon Thorne had been obstinate. The cell door had been locked on her. Fortunately the night had been peaceful, broken only by the snoring of the prisoner at the bottom of the passage.

When Lee Baxter and the sheriff walked into Judge Barratt's comfortable home on the outskirts of Grass Valley, leaving their horses tied to the rail beside the neat, white picket fence, Lee had a plan in mind. He would put it to the judge.

The two men sank into deep leather chairs and Judge Barratt pointed to a box of cigars on the mahogany table. 'Help yourselves, gentlemen. And would you like a drink?' He reached out for a glass decanter and some glasses that lay on a silver tray. The amber

127

liquid gleamed richly as Judge Barratt poured three glasses. He looked a severe man, with eyes that rarely smiled, but he had a deep respect for the law he administered and a large measure of understanding of human failings.

'Now this girl ... this Anita Graham. Of course, I know her ... Gilbert Graham did good work in this community for years, although ...' The judge shook his head. 'He is failing now. She is his daughter and he should exercise more control over her, but that doesn't seem possible.'

'She can't stay in that jail, sir,' Lee burst out. 'How often do we have to jail women in this town? When we release her, the other women in Grass Valley will talk about her for a long time.'

'She is concealing the whereabouts of that map,' grated Jon Thorne. 'It isn't her property. What's the ruling on this thing, Judge?'

'Treasure trove belongs to the finder, although in some states one-fourth of the value is requested by the state. Now, in this instance, the question of the moment is the ownership of the map. It was, apparently, made by one Simon Dawson from ancient documents—so much you have told me, Sheriff Thorne. With the death of the two Dawsons, this map belongs to no one person until the question of heirs is investigated. The map, if it should be found, will have to be kept in legal custody. That might be for a long time.'

'And after that, sir?'

'The treasure is there for the finding.' A slight smile spread over the judge's face. 'Treasure seeking is notoriously tricky, gentlemen. Old maps are sometimes inaccurate. Landmarks alter with the passing of years. I have read accounts of many treasure-seeking expeditions that have proved futile even after months of exploration.'

'I've got an idea,' Lee put in swiftly. 'Something I've been thinking about, sir. If we give the girl her freedom, she'll make an attempt to recover that map. We can be watching her every move and with a bit of luck be right behind her when she picks up the map. That's better than keeping her in jail.'

Judge Barratt nodded, his expression betraying interest. 'It might work, although the idea is a trifle irregular.'

'It's crazy!' exploded Jon Thorne. 'Who the hell is gonna keep tabs on her?'

The judge leaned forward to knock ash from his cigar. He smiled. 'Who better than our friend, Deputy Baxter? In fact, as it is his idea, I place the girl in his charge. He will be responsible for her behaviour.'

But Jon Thorne had doubts. 'A deputy's time has to be paid for, Judge Barratt. We're short on lawmen in this town as it is.'

'That is true. But maybe the affair of this extraordinary map may be cleared up faster

129

than we think. In any case, it's better than keeping a girl in the town jail, with all the gossip it will entail. So, Deputy Baxter, your idea has brought you fresh responsibilities. You will watch every move of that girl once she is free. If she attempts to seek the hiding place of that map, by all means let her carry on—and use your initiative to get the map.'

With mixed feelings Lee and the sheriff went to the girl and told her about part of the judge's decision. They made no reference to the missing map and they certainly gave no hint that they intended to trick the girl.

'You're free to go,' grunted Jon Thorne. 'Judge Barratt says you can't stay here—ain't good for you and it ain't good for us. There's only one thing. Lee Baxter is responsible for your behaviour. You do something stupid and he'll be in trouble.'

Anita laughed. 'Thank you for my freedom. But I don't need a guardian—and certainly not Deputy Lee Baxter!' She flicked them a cold glance. 'I'll just go home and have a bath. Then I'll be a good girl—for a half-Ute!'

She did go home, to be welcomed by her father at the door. She filled a wooden tub with hot water, got some scented soap and a large sponge and then, locking the door, enjoyed the luxury of a long bath. An hour later she was sitting with her father, ostensibly reading a novel by Charles Dickens but actually wondering at his thoughts. He had a newspaper and he did not question her.

Lee Baxter almost regretted his suggestion that the girl should be allowed her freedom. He had to watch the house that night. Jon Thorne had said he'd better stick with the chore twenty-four hours a day. So Lee walked up the hill and sat against a tree.

*   *   *

In Grass Valley some odd rumours had made the rounds of the saloons, and also in parlours where women gathered in the afternoon to drink tea. But it was the men in the saloons who were really interested in the story that old Gilbert Graham's daughter had found the map of the treasure trove in the hills. It was a fact that she had been placed in the jailhouse. And now she was free.

Two hardcases whose brains were addled by whisky had it all figured out. 'That gal found the treasure, I've been told. It's there . . . right up there in them blamed hills where it's always been . . .'

'Then how come she ain't got it? How come she got shoved in jail?'

'That's just to protect her, pardner. See? Ain't good for a girl to walk around knowing all that. But I reckon there'll be some galoots ridin' up there tomorrow with her—if we don't do something about it.' A crafty unshaven face stared into his companion's mouthful of bad teeth. 'You and me, Bert, could do with some luck. We need dinero bad, don't we?'

'Sure do.' Bert was a heavy man who had been in every kind of grief since his father had kicked him out at fifteen. Seething with grudges that would never be satisfied, he saw everything in terms of revenge. 'We could get hold of that girl—is that your idea, Ezra? Make her talk, huh? Sure seems easy to me—only a damn girl . . .'

'She's part-Ute. Ain't no need to treat her kindly.' Ezra laughed nastily. 'No Ute was ever worth spittin' on. C'mon, we've had enough of this rot-gut.'

They went into the dark street, two devils with greed stirring their brains to action. They carried heavy Colts in scuffed holsters. They thought they'd need horses so they went along to the ramshackle livery where they kept their animals. In the saddle, they rode around town, ignoring the flow of people, hell-bent on one idea only.

They knew where the girl lived, but it would be stupid to ride up and make a lot of noise. So the horses were left in an alley at the edge of town, with the thought that they could get to them quickly if they needed to leave in a hurry. And if they had this girl who knew so much about the treasure, they might want to ride out.

They reckoned without a watchful deputy. This detail had not been pointed out to them in the saloon.

Lee Baxter saw the two dark shapes only momentarily as they moved up the hill and ran to the side of the house. He moved from the tree bole as if jerked by invisible strings. He broke into a run as the two men disappeared around the gable end of the house.

For the girl and her father the first warning of trouble came when they heard someone try to open the rear door. Anita heard low curses and knew she was in danger.

She ran to her father. 'Where is the gun? What happened to the gun you kept on the wall? It's gone...'

He looked at her and trembled. 'Guns are bad things, Anita. The day will arrive when there is no need for weapons. I had a man take the gun away.' He got to his feet. 'But what is happening?'

'We've got visitors, Father. The kind that understand only brute force. Some scum from the saloons, I'd say.'

As another fresh hammering came on the door and the planks crackled under the impact of a boot, she wished Baxter would appear. And Lee Baxter came around the house just as the door broke with the weight of two men against it. The two hardcases staggered as the door gave. They were regaining their balance when

133

Lee jumped into view, his gun out.

'Hold it, you two!'

The two men clawed for their guns.

Lee triggered twice. The two other guns didn't even fire. Fingers that were on the verge of jerking triggers suddenly went nerveless. Falling, the men tried to clutch at their chests, as if this would alleviate the hellish pain. Then, strength ebbing from their lungs, they fell to the ground.

Lee stared at them for a long time, then he holstered his gun as the girl edged slowly around the broken door. She looked grimly at the bodies and then at Lee.

'Are you all right?' she asked. It was no formality; there was real anxiety in her breathed words.

'I'm in one piece,' Lee said.

'These men? Who—?'

'I've seen them in the saloons a few times. They're real hardcases, Anita. I'd say they've heard about the treasure.'

Her hands went to her face. 'I wish I'd never heard of the cache—never saw Magruder—or talked Jesse into helping me.'

'Don't blame yourself, Anita. We all make mistakes—I've made plenty in the past. You won't ever find me throwing blame at you.'

'I—I think I'd better tell you everything about that map,' she said, then her eyes widened in disbelief and seemed to be focused beyond him.

Too late he turned, his hand on the butt of his gun.

The man in the garb of a poor Chinaman brought the lump of wood down hard on Lee Baxter's head, knocking his hat flat. Lee fell, and he took three swift paces to the girl's side and poked her ribs with his derringer. 'Don't cry out! I could kill you—or better still, kill this deputy. You wouldn't like that...'

CHAPTER TWELVE

DEFEATED!

He took her to a dark, cold, cellar-like place and tied her in a chair. She watched this man in the garb of a Chinese labourer, puzzled.

'Who are you?' she asked. He had pushed her along with the gun in her back, all the way from her father's house, leaving Lee Baxter unconscious. They had moved through back alleys, avoiding the main street. They had met nobody; the nearest passerby had been many yards away. Her captor had poked hard with the gun, a warning not to cry out. And then they had dived into this big old barn-like structure near the stockyards. A door had clanged behind him; then he had pulled up a heavy trap-door, pointed the gleaming little gun at her and hissed, 'Down there. Don't try anything foolish!'

She had known he wasn't Chinese. His tall figure—when he discarded the hunch to his shoulders—reminded her of someone. She was still thinking along these lines when he completed the bindings around her legs and hands. He stood back, his wrinkled face carved in a grin.

'Even if you scream you won't be heard,' he

said, and the educated tone of voice told her all she wanted to know.

'Beeson! You—you are mad. This crazy disguise—'

'I can move around town like this,' he said. 'It's the work of a master, a man who—but enough of that. Suffice to say that nobody in Grass Valley looks twice at a poor Chink. I've tried it in the streets. Mind you, I can't go back to my office ... but when I get that map I'll have a venture on my hands better than all the property deals that could come my way if I lived to be a hundred.'

'You're out of your mind!' she flung at him. 'Nobody can work at finding that treasure now without attracting a ton of attention. How are you going to do it?'

'I'll do it,' he said firmly.

'You've avoided the question,' she taunted, 'because you hate to face up to the fact that you're a wanted man. You can't move around freely—order gear—shift horses—hire labour. Why, look at you—a comical scarecrow of a man—a lowly Chinese labourer...'

'Damn you!' Some of his old arrogance flushed through his disguise. He struck out at the girl, his hand slapping her face.

She recovered. 'You fool! I'll never tell you where to find the map. I'll die before I'll let you win.'

'You said that the last time—up in the hills.'

'I meant it.'

'You dirty little half-breed,' he sneered. 'In the end you'll be glad to tell me where you put that map.'

'You'll be hanged,' she said. 'Carl Beeson, hanging in a public place for folks to stare at. You're a murderer!'

He moved away from her, back to the steps leading to the floor above. 'I'm going for a few little items that will make you talk. By sunup you *will* talk—and you'll tell me the truth. I'll know it if you try to lie—you won't be able to fool me. You'll tell the truth because it will be the only thing that will get you any mercy. As for this old cellar, the ceiling is made of stone slabs—it's sound-proof. You won't be heard when you scream in agony and no one will arrive to help you.'

And with that he was gone. The trap-door thudded into place. She glanced at the roof above her; saw the solid stone and knew he was right. She might as well save her breath.

All the same she struggled against the ropes that bound her ankles and wrists. There might not be much time; he'd be back quickly. She fought the tight bindings so fiercely that the rough fibres bit into her flesh. In that moment, in the wan yellow light from the lamp he'd left lit, she was a strange figure. She had discarded the buckskin dress after she'd had the hot-water bath, and had changed into a simple gingham dress. With her hair newly plaited, her eyes wide and frightened, she looked a lovely picture—but helpless and in danger from a man whose mind was crazed with the thought of tremendous wealth.

★   ★   ★

Lee Baxter got to his feet and staggered around. he held onto the splintered doorpost and looked dazedly for some seconds at the two dead saloon bums. Things came back into his brain that made sense. He could remember Anita standing before him saying. 'Are you all right?' Then the sense of impending danger ... but too late. Something had thudded onto his head. Probably his hat had saved him from a cracked skull.

Logical thoughts quickly swimming into his brain, he looked up as Gilbert Graham showed in the broken doorway, a frightened old man.

'Anita ... where the hell is she?' Lee demanded, hand on his gun.

But he knew that Anita was gone. Somebody had taken her away. That damned map again! The very thing he was supposed to guard her against had happened, and all he had to show for it was a lump on his head and a headache. First the two saloon bums, then another man. Who else but Beeson?

Lee Baxter strode through the house,

knowing Anita wasn't there even as he wasted the time searching. Then he went down to Grass Valley's main street. He had to report to Sheriff Thorne. The man would be at home. On the way to this painful duty, he'd keep an eye open for anything suspicious, but he had the sickening feeling that Anita was on a fast-moving horse, heading out of town, threatened by Beeson. The man couldn't move around Grass Valley in the open without being observed by someone.

Jon Thorne owned a fine, rambling clapboard house on the west side of town, where cottonwoods gave shelter from the winter winds. Lee strode on grimly, aware of every tiny sound and movement in the night, cursing Beeson. Knowing that every passing second counted, he darted through an alley that offered a short-cut that would take him past the stockyards.

He was striding like a giant when he heard the clip-clop of a horse's hoofs. The animal wasn't being ridden—he'd know that sound anywhere. It was a horse shifting position. Lee halted, then stared at the old wooden building close by. He saw the loose boards, a window that was shattered and the peeling paint that said, BREWERY. As he stared he heard the sounds the horse made. He'd been in the town long enough to know that this place was abandoned.

His brain was sending jagged warning flashes of light through his head. Somewhere behind his eyes he saw the shadowy man who had hit him. The shadow flashed on and off, like a hurricane lamp in the night. His brain was warning him . . . A man in queer clothes . . . a shadow . . .

Lee Baxter obeyed the blind hunch. He walked to the old door in the side of the building. He pushed it open and slid in, a shadow himself, part of the darkness.

He heard the horse again but couldn't see the animal. Then there was another sound, regular, the sound of a man's boots—but with a difference. The noise was wooden, as if someone was knocking two bits of wood together. He heard it again, a queer tapping sound.

Lee knew there was something strange about these noises in the night. He sidled along the plank wall, feeling his way through the gloom. He heard the sounds of a horse's breathing; noises that suggested a man was attending to the animal.

Lee took four clear strides through the darkness, sure he would blunder into the horse and the man. But he misjudged the distance and had to halt, for the gloom was so impenetrable he felt momentarily lost.

He'd been heard. He knew it. There was a long silence and then the grating sound of a

141

match being struck. Yellow light flared. Lee Baxter found himself staring at the odd figure of a hunched Chinaman in a voluminous smock and battered straw hat.

'Who the hell are you?' Lee demanded.

The other man did not hesitate. 'I am Chou Sing...'

In the match's light the two men stared at each other. Then Beeson felt for his derringer. He'd played out the charade long enough. He poked the derringer through an opening in his smock.

Lee Baxter leaped like a mountain cat, propelling himself at the man's legs. He didn't want to kill the man—not until he knew what had happened to Anita.

The derringer spat flame into the night, but by then Lee had rammed into the man and the small bullet spewed wide into the darkness. He smashed into the other man, colliding with the old horse that stood with drooping head. As Lee and the other man crashed to the floor, wooden sandals thudded against the floor. Lee wasted no time or mercy on this man, knowing he was the one who'd struck him at Anita's house. He rammed a fist into the face, guessing distance with complete accuracy in the darkness. He felt the man slump. Lee hit him again just to make sure.

The man was out. Lee felt around in the gloom and located the box of matches on the floor. He struck one of the long-stemmed sticks into light and looked in amazement at the yellowed face beneath him.

A Chinaman in this old brewery building—a horse and a toy-like gun. Then Lee looked closer at the yellow face and the black hair. He rubbed hard at the man's cheek and yellow paint came away. Underneath was pinkish skin.

It was ten minutes later that he made Carl Beeson talk, and that was only because he hit the man repeatedly with the palm of his hand, jarring teeth and making him cry out with pain. 'Come on, Beeson—what have you done with Anita?'

'She's in the cellar,' muttered Beeson sullenly.

Dazed, uncomprehending, unwilling to accept the reality of defeat, Carl Beeson began talking like a man pushed to the limits of his sanity. He was pleading, babbling, talking of a treasure. In his confusion, he showed Lee Baxter the trap-door.

Lee pushed Beeson ahead into the cellar where Anita struggled against her bonds and a lamp gave yellow light.

He had no trouble in dealing with Carl Beeson. The man had lost all fight and talked on incessantly, stupidly. Lee used the rope he cut from Anita to bind the man's hands behind his back.

Some time later, when Beeson was in jail and

Anita safely home, Lee went to see her.

'The map,' he said gently. 'You'll tell us where to find it?'

She nodded. 'I've been a fool, Lee. Yes, we can find the map again...'

He held her hands. 'If the gold and other valuables are found, the money will be shared—I'm sure of that. The Ute tribe will be helped. Maybe Grass Valley will benefit, with new schools for kids and a hospital. Maybe it'll be a good thing, Anita ... but it's too big for one person. And it will take a lot of work to locate—digging—looking—weeks in the hills...'

'I'll give the map to Judge Barratt,' she said, then she looked at him with clear eyes. 'I've been silly—a mixed-up girl with Ute blood.'

'You're the loveliest creature in this territory,' he told her. 'And you can forget the mixed-up thing from now on. You're a very real person, Anita.'

She smiled, reaching out to him. 'You're not corrupted by thoughts of vast wealth, Lee. What is it you want most in life?'

'Peace of mind.' He grinned. 'And I want you, Anita. I aim to marry you.'

Photoset, printed and bound in Great Britain by REDWOOD PRESS LIMITED, Melksham, Wiltshire